A Counterfeit Presentment

&

The Parlour Car

William D. Howells

Contents

I. BARTLETT and CUMMINGS...7
II. GENERAL WYATT, BARTLETT, AND CUMMINGS. 14
III MRS. WYATT, CONSTANCE, and the others. 15
IV. BARTLETT AND CUMMINGS. 17
V. CUMMINGS and GENERAL WYATT. 19
VI. CUMMINGS and BARTLETT...25
VII. GENERAL WYATT, CUMMINGS, and BARTLETT.................................30
VIII. CONSTANCE, MRS. WYATT, and the others. 33

II. DISTINCTIONS AND DIFFERENCES. 34
I. CONSTANCE and MRS. WYATT. 34
II. BARTLETT and CONSTANCE, ...39
III. MRS. WYATT and CONSTANCE. 46
IV. GENERAL WYATT, CONSTANCE, and MRS. WYATT. 48
V. CONSTANCE and MRS. WYATT; then BARTLETT. 50

III. DISSOLVING VIEWS. 52
I. GENERAL WYATT and MRS. WYATT..52
II. BARTLETT, GENERAL WYATT, and MRS, WYATT.................................55
III. CONSTANCE, BARTLETT, and GENERAL WYATT. 57
IV. MRS. WYATT and GENERAL WYATT. 69
V. BARTLETT and CONSTANCE 70

IV. NOT AT ALL LIKE...73
I. BABTLETT and CUMMINGS..73
II. CONSTANCE, MRS. WYATT, BABTLETT, and CUMMINGS. 79
III. BARTLETT and CUMMINGS..82

ROMANCE...86
  I. 86
  II. 86
  III. 86
  IV. 87

V. GENERAL WYATT, MRS. WYATT, CONSTANCE, and BARTLETT. 92

THE PARLOUR CAR. 98
A FARCE. 98

A COUNTERFEIT PRESENTMENT
& THE PARLOUR CAR

BY

William D. Howells

A COUNTERFEIT PRESENTMENT.

(The Scene is always in the Parlour of the Ponkwasset Hotel.)

I.
BARTLETT and CUMMINGS.

ON a lovely day in September, at that season when the most sentimental of the young maples have begun to redden along the hidden courses of the meadow streams, and the elms, with a sudden impression of despair in their languor, betray flecks of yellow on the green of their pendulous boughs,—on such a day at noon, two young men enter the parlour of the Ponkwasset Hotel, and deposit about the legs of the piano the burdens they have been carrying: a camp-stool namely, a field-easel, a closed box of colours, and a canvas to which, apparently, some portion of reluctant nature has just been transferred. These properties belong to one of the young men, whose general look and bearing readily identify him as their owner : he has a quick, somewhat furtive eye, a full brown beard, and hair that falls in a careless mass down his forehead, which, as he dries it with his handkerchief, sweeping the hair aside, shows broad and white; his figure is firm and square, without heaviness, and in his movement as well as in his face there is something of stubbornness, with a suggestion of arrogance. The other, who has evidently borne his share of the common burdens from a sense of good comradeship, has nothing of the painter in him, nor anything of this painter's peculiar temperament: he has a very abstracted look and a dark, dreaming eye: he is pale, and does not look strong, The painter flings himself into a rocking chair and draws a long breath.

Cummings (for that is the name of the slighter man, who remains standing as he speaks).—"It's warm, isn't it?" His gentle face evinces a curious and kindly interest in his friend's sturdy demonstrations of fatigue.

Bartlett—"Yes, hot—confoundedly." He rubs his handkerchief vigorously across his forehead, and then looks down at his dusty shoes, with apparently no mind to molest them in their dustiness. "The idea of people going back to town in this weather! However, I'm glad they're such asses; it gives me free scope here. Every time I don't hear some young woman banging on that piano, I fall into transports of joy."

Cummings, smiling.—"And after to-day you won't be bothered even with me."

Bartlett.—"Oh, I shall rather miss you, you know. I like somebody to contradict."

Cummings.—"You can contradict the ostler."

Bartlett—"No, I can't. They've sent him away; and I believe you're going to carry off the last of the table-girls with you in the stage to-morrow. The landlord and his wife are to run the concern themselves the rest of the fall. Poor old fellow! The hard times have made lean pickings for him this year. His house wasn't full in the height of the season, and it's been pretty empty since."

Cummings.—"I wonder he doesn't shut up altogether."

Bartlett.—"Well, there are a good many-transients, as they call them, at this time of year,—fellows who drive over from the little hill-towns with their girls in buggies, and take dinner and supper; then there are picnics from the larger places, ten and twelve miles off, that come to the grounds on the pond, and he always gets something out of them. And as long as he can hope for anything else, my eight dollars a week are worth hanging on to. Yes, I think I shall stay here all through October. I've got no orders, and it's cheap. Besides, I've managed to get on confidential terms with the local scenery; I thought we should like each other last summer, and I feel now that we're ready to swear eternal friendship. I shall do some fairish work here, yet. Phew!" He mops his forehead again, and springing out of his chair he goes up to the canvas, which he has faced to the wall, and turning it about retires some paces, and with a swift, worried glance at the windows falls to considering it critically.

Cummings.—"You've done some fairish work already, if I'm any judge." He comes to his friend's side, as if to get his effect of the picture. "I don't believe the spirit of a graceful elm that just begins to feel the approach of autumn was ever better interpreted. There is something tremendously tragical to me in the thing. It makes me think of some lovely and charming girl, all grace and tenderness, who finds the first grey hair in her head. I should call that picture The First Grey Hair."

Bartlett, with unheeding petulance.—"The whole thing's too infernally brown! I beg your pardon, Cummings : what were you saying? Go on! I like your prattle about pictures; I do, indeed. I like to see how far you art-cultured fellows can miss all that was in a poor devil's mind when he was at work. But I'd rather you'd senti-mentalise my pictures than moralise them. If there's anything that makes me quite limp, it's to have an allegory discovered in one of my poor stupid old landscapes. But The First Grey Hair isn't bad, really. And a good, senseless, sloppy name like that often sells a picture."

Cummings.—"You're brutal, Bartlett. I don't believe your pictures would own you, if they had their way about it."

Bartlett—"And I wouldn't own them if I had mine. I've got about forty that I wish somebody else owned—and I had the money for them; but we seem insepa-rable. Glad you're going to-morrow? You are a good fellow, Cummings, and I am a brute. Come, I'll make a great concession to friendship : it struck me, too, while I was at work on that elm, that it was something like—an old girl!" Bartlett laughs, and catching his friend by either shoulder, twists him about in his strong clutch, while he looks him merrily in the face. "I'm not a poet, old fellow; and sometimes I think I ought to have been a painter and glazier instead of a mere painter. I believe it would have paid better."

Cummings.—"Bartlett, I hate to have you talk in that way."

Bartlett.—"Oh, I know it's a stale kind."

Cummings.—"It's worse than stale. It's destructive. A man can soon talk him-self out of heart with his better self. You can end by really being as sordid-minded and hopeless and low-purposed as you pretend to be. It's insanity."

Bartlett—"Good! I've had my little knock on the head, you know. I don't deny being cracked. But I've a method in my madness."

Cummings.—"They all have. But it's a very poor method; and I don't believe you could say just what yours is. You think because a girl on whom you set your fancy—it's nonsense to pretend it was your heart—found out she didn't like you as well as she thought, and honestly told you so in good time, that your wisest course is to take up that rôle of misanthrope which begins with yourself and leaves people to imagine how low an opinion you have of the rest of mankind."

Bartlett.—"My dear fellow, you know I always speak well of that young lady. I've invariably told you that she behaved in the handsomest manner. She even expressed the wish—I distinctly remember being struck by the novelty of the wish at the time—that we should remain friends. You misconceive"—

Cummings.—"How many poor girls have been jilted who don't go about doing misanthropy, but mope at home and sorrow and sicken over their wrong in secret,—a wrong that attacks not merely their pride, but their life itself. Take the case I was telling you of : did you ever hear of anything more atrocious? And do you compare this little sting to your vanity with a death-blow like that?"

Bartlett—"It's quite impossible to compute the number of jilted girls who take the line you describe. But if it were within the scope of arithmetic, I don't know that a billion of jilted girls would comfort me or reform me. I never could regard myself in that abstract way—a mere unit on one side or other of the balance. My little personal snub goes on rankling beyond the reach of statistical consolation. But even if there were any edification in the case of the young lady in Paris, she's too far off to be an example for me. Take some jilted girl nearer home, Cummings, if you want me to go round sickening and sorrowing in secret. I don't believe you can find any. Women are much tougher about the pericardium than we give them credit for, my dear fellow,—much. I don't see why it should hurt a woman more than a man to be jilted. We shall never truly philosophise this important matter till we regard women with something of the fine penetration and impartiality with which they regard each other. Look at the stabs they give and take—they would kill men! And the graceful ferocity with which they despatch any of their number who happens to be down is quite unexampled in natural history. How much do you suppose her lady friends have left of that poor girl whose case wrings your foolish bosom all the way from Paris? I don't believe so much as a boot-button. Why, even your correspondent—a very lively woman, by the way—can't conceal under all her indignation her little satisfaction that so proud a girl as Miss What's-her-name should have been jilted. Of course, she doesn't say it."

Cummings hotly.—"No, she doesn't say it, and it's not to your credit to imagine it."

Bartlett, with a laugh.—"Oh, I don't ask any praise for the discovery. You deserve praise for not making it. It does honour to your good heart. Well, don't be vexed, old fellow. And in trying to improve me on this little point—a weak point, I'll allow, with me—do me the justice to remember that I didn't flaunt my misanthropy, as you call it, in your face; I didn't force my confidence upon you."

Cummings, with compunction.—"I didn't mean to hurt your feelings, Bartlett."

Bartlett—"Well, you haven't. It's all right."

Cummings, with anxious concern.—"I wish I could think so."

Bartlett, dryly.—"You have my leave—my request, in fact." He takes a turn about the room, thrusting his fingers through the hair on his forehead, and lettting it fall in a heavy tangle, and then pulling at either side of his parted beard. In facing away from one of the sofas at the end of the room, he looks back over his shoulder at it, falters, wheels about, and picks up from it a lady's shawl and hat. "Hallo!" He lets the shawl fall again into picturesque folds on the sofa. "This is the spoil of no local beauty, Cummings. Look here; I don't understand this. There has been an arrival."

Cummings, joining his friend in contemplation of the hat and shawl : "Yes; it's an arrival beyond all question. Those are a lady's things. I should think that was a Paris hat." They remain looking at the things some moments in silence.

Bartlett—"How should a Paris hat get here? I know the landlord wasn't expecting it. But it can't be going to stay; it 5s here through some caprice. It may be a transient of quality, but it's a transient. I suppose we shall see the young woman belonging to it at dinner." He sets the hat on his fist, and holds it at arm's length from him. "What a curious thing it is about clothes "—

Cummings.—"Don't, Bartlett, don't!"

Bartlett—"Why?"

Cummings.—"I don't know. It makes me feel as if you were offering an indignity to the young lady herself."

Bartlett.—"You express my idea exactly; This frippery has not only the girl's personality but her very spirit in it. This hat looks like her; you can infer the whole woman from it, body and soul. It has a conscious air, and so has the shawl, as if they had been eavesdropping and had understood everything we were saying. They know all about my heart-break, and so will she as soon as she puts them on; she will be interested in me. The hat's in good taste, isn't it?"

Cummings, with sensitive reverence for the millinery which his friend handles so daringly.—"Exquisite it seems to me; but I don't know about such things."

Bartlett.—"Neither do I; but I feel about them. Besides, a painter and glazier sees some things that are hidden from even a progressive minister. Let us interpret the lovely being from her hat. This knot of pale-blue flowers betrays her a blonde; this lace, this mass of silky, fluffy, cob-webby what-do-you-call-it, and this delicate straw fabric show that she is slight; a stout woman would kill it, or die in the attempt. And I fancy—here pure inspiration comes to my aid—that she is tallish. I'm afraid of her! No—wait! The shawl has something to say. "He takes it up and catches it across his arm, where he scans it critically. "I don't know that I understand the shawl, exactly. It proves her of a good height,—a short woman wouldn't, or had better not, wear a shawl,—but this black colour : should you think it was mourning? Have we a lovely young widow among us?"

Cwmmings.—"I don't see how it could go with the hat, if it were."

Bartlett.—"True; the hat is very pensive in tone, but it isn't mourning. This shawl's very light, it's very warm; I construct from it a pretty invalid." He lets the shawl slip down his arm to his hand, and flings it back upon the sofa. "We return from the young lady's heart to her brain—where she carries her sentiments. She has a nice taste in perfumes, Cummings : faintest violet; that goes with the blue. Of what religion is a young lady who uses violet, my reverend friend?"

Cummings.—"Bartlett, you're outrageous. Put down that hat!"

Bartlett—"No, seriously. What is her little æsthetic specialty? Does she sketch? Does she scribble? Tell me, thou wicked hat, does she flirt? Come; out with the vows that you have heard poured into the shelly ear under this knot of pale-blue flowers! Where be her gibes now, her gambols, her flashes of merriment? Now get you to my lady's chamber, and tell her, let her paint an inch thick, to this favour she must come; make her laugh at that. Dost thou think, Horatio Cummings, Cleopatra looked o' this fashion? And smelt so?"—he presses the knot of artificial flowers to his moustache—"Pah!" He tosses the hat on the sofa and walks away.

Cummings.—"Bartlett, this is atrocious, I protest"—

Bartlett—"Well, give me up, I tell you." He returns, and takes his friend by the shoulders, as before, and laughs. "I'm not worth your refined pains. I might be good, at a pinch, but I never could be truly ladylike."

Cummings.—"You like to speak an infinite deal of nothing, don't you?"

Bartlett.—"It's the only thing that makes conversation." As he releases Cummings, and turns away from him, in the doorway he confronts an elderly gentleman, whose white hair and white moustache give distinction to his handsome florid face. There is something military in his port, as he stands immoveably erect upon the threshold, his left hand lodged in the breast of his frock-coat, and his head carried with an officer-like air of command. His visage grows momently redder and redder, and his blue eyes blaze upon Bartlett with a fascinated glare that briefly preludes the burst of fury with which he advances toward him

II.
GENERAL WYATT, BARTLETT, AND CUMMINGS.

General Wyatt.—"You infernal scoundrel! What are you doing here?" He raises his stick at Bartlett, who remains motionlessly frowning in wrathful bewilderment, his strong hand knotting itself into, a fist where it hangs at his side, while Cummings starts toward them in dismay, with his hand raised to interpose. "Didn't I tell you if I ever set eyes on you again, you villain—didn't I warn you that if you ever crossed my path, you"—He stops with a violent self-arrest, and lets his stick drop as he throws up both his hands in amaze, "Good Heavens! It's a mistake! I beg your pardon, sir; I do, indeed." He lets fall his hands, and stands staring into Bartlett's face with his illusion apparently not fully dispelled. "A mistake, sir, a mistake. I was misled, sir, by the most prodigious resemblance"—At the sound of voices in the corridor without, he turns from Bartlett, and starts back toward the door.

A Voice, very sweet and weak, without.—"I left them in here, I think."

Another Voice.—"You must sit down, Constance, and let me look."

The First Voice.—"Oh, they'll be here."

General Wyatt, in a loud and anxious tone.—"Margaret, Margaret! Don't bring Constance in here! Go away!" At the moment he reaches the door by which he came in, two ladies in black enter the parlour by the other door, the younger leaning weakly on the arm of the elder, and with a languidly drooping head letting her eyes rove listlessly about over the chairs and sofas. With an abrupt start at sight of Bartlett, who has mechanically turned toward them, the elder lady arrests their movement.

III
MRS. WYATT, CONSTANCE, and the others.

Mrs. Wyatt.—"Oh, in mercy's name!" The young lady wearily lifts her eyes; they fall upon Bartlett's face, and a low cry parts her lips as she approaches a pace or two nearer, releasing her arm from her mother's.

Constance.—"Ah!" She stops; her thin hands waver before her face, as if to clear or to obstruct her vision, and all at once she sinks forward into a little slender heap upon the floor, almost at Bartlett's feet. He instantly drops upon his knees beside her, and stoops over her to lift her up.

Mrs. Wyatt.—"Don't touch her, you cruel wretch! Your touch is poison; the sight of you is murder!" Kneeling on the other side of her daughter, she sets both her hands against his breast and pushes him back.

General Wyatt.—"Margaret, stop! Look! Look at him again! It isn't he !"

Mrs. Wyatt.—"Not he? Don't tell me! What?" She clutches Bartlett's arm, and scans his face with dilating eyes. "Oh! it isn't, it isn't! But go away,—go away, all the same! You may be an innocent man, but she would perish in your presence. Keep your hands from her, sir! If your wicked heart is not yet satisfied with your wicked work—Excuse me; I don't know what I'm saying! But if you have any pity in your faithless soul—I—oh, speak for me, James, and send him—implore him to go away!" She bows her face over her daughter's pale visage, and sobs.

General Wyatt.—"Sir, you must pardon us, and have the great goodness to be patient. You have a right to feel yourself aggrieved by what has happened, but no wrong is meant,—no offence. You must be so kind as to go away. I will make you all the needed apologies and explanations." He stoops over his daughter, as Bartlett, in a sort of daze, rises from his knees and retires a few steps. "I beg your pardon, sir,"—

addressing himself to Cummings,—"will you help me a moment?" Cummings, with delicate sympathy and tenderness, lifts the arms of the insensible girl to her father's neck, and assists the General to rise with his burden. "Thanks! She's hardly heavier, poor child, than a ghost." The tears stand in his eyes, as he gathers her closer to him and kisses her wan cheek. "Sir,"—as he moves away he speaks to Bartlett,—"do me the favour to remain here till I can return to offer you reparation." He makes a stately effort to bow to Bartlett in leaving the room, while his wife, who follows with the young lady's hat and shawl, looks back at the painter with open abhorrence.

IV.
BARTLETT AND CUMMINGS.

Bartlett, turning to his friend from the retreating group on which he has kept his eyes steadfastly fixed,—"Where are their keepers?" He is pale with suppressed rage.

Cummings.—"Their keepers? "

Bartlett, savagely.—"Yes! Have they escaped from them, or is it one of the new ideas to let lunatics go about the country alone? If that old fool hadn't dropped his stick, I'd have knocked him over that table in another instant. And that other old maniac,—what did she mean by pushing me back in that way? How do you account for this thing, Cummings? What do you make of it?"

Cummings.—"I don't know, upon my word. There seems to be some mystery,— some painful mystery. But the gentleman will be back directly, I suppose, and"—

Bartlett, crushing his hat over his eyes.—"I'll leave you to receive him and his mystery. I've had enough of both." He moves toward the door.

Cummings, detaining him.—"Bartlett, you're surely not going away?"

Bartlett.—"Yes, I am!"

Cummings.—"But he'll be here in a moment. He said he would come back and satisfy the claim which you certainly have to an explanation."

Bartlett, furiously.—"Claim? I've a perfect Alabama Claim to an explanation. He can't satisfy it; he shall not try. It's a little too much to expect me to be satisfied with anything he can say after what's passed. Get out of the way, Cummings, or I'll put you on top of the piano."

Cummings.—"You may throw me out of the window, if you like, but not till I've done my best to keep you here. It's a shame, it's a crime to go away. You talk about lunatics: you're a raving madman, yourself. Have one glimmer of reason, do;

and see what you're about. It's a mistake; it's a misunderstanding. It's his right, it's your duty, to have it cleared up. Come, you've a conscience, Bartlett, and a clean one. Don't give way to your abominable temper. What? You won't stay? Bartlett, I blush for you!"

Bartlett—"Blush unseen, then!" He thrusts Cummings aside and pushes furiously from the room. Cummings looks into the corridor after him, and then returns, panting, to the piano, and mechanically rearranges the things at his feet; he walks nervously away, and takes some turns up and down the room, looking utterly bewildered, and apparently uncertain whether to go or stay. But he has decided upon the only course really open to him by sinking down into one of the armchairs, when General Wyatt appears at the threshold of the door on the right of the piano. Cummings rises and comes forward in great embarrassment to meet him.

V.
CUMMINGS and GENERAL WYATT.

General Wyatt, with a look of surprise at not seeing Bartlett.—"The other gentleman"—

Cummings.—"My friend has gone out. I hope he will return soon. He has—I hardly know what to say to you, sir. He has done himself great injustice; but it was natural that under the circumstances"—

General Wyatt, with hurt pride.—"Perfectly. I should have lost my temper, too; but I think I should have waited at the request—the prayer of an older man. I don't mind his temper; the other villain had no temper. Sir, am I right in addressing you as the Rev. Arthur Cummings?"

Cummings.—"My name is Arthur Cummings. I am a minister."

General Wyatt.—"I thought I was not mistaken this time. I heard you preach last Sunday in Boston; and I know your cousin, Major Cummings of the 34th Artillery. I am General Wyatt."

Cummings, with a start of painful surprise and sympathy.—"General Wyatt?"

General Wyatt, keenly.—"Your cousin has mentioned me to you?"

Cummings.—"Yes,—oh yes, certainly; certainly, very often, General Wyatt. But"—endeavouring to recover himself—"your name is known to us all, and honoured. I—I am glad to see you back; I—understood you were in Paris."

General Wyatt, with fierce defiance.—"I was in Paris three weeks ago." Some moments of awkward silence ensue, during which General Wyatt does not relax his angry attitude.

Cummings, finally.—"I am sorry my friend is not here to meet you. I ought to say, in justice to him, that his hasty temper does great wrong to his heart and judgment."

General Wyatt.—"Why, yes, sir; so does mine—so does mine,"

Cummings, with a respectful smile lost upon the General.--—"And I know that he will certainly be grieved in this instance to have yielded to it."

General Wyatt, with sudden meekness.—

"I hope so, sir. But I am not altogether sorry that he has done it. I have not only an explanation but a request to make,—a very great and strange favour to ask,—and I am not sure that I should be able to treat him civilly enough throughout an entire interview to ask it properly." Cummings listens with an air of attentive respect, but makes, to this strange statement, no response other than a look of question, while the General pokes about on the carpet at his feet with the point of his stick for a moment before he brings it resolutely down upon the floor with a thump, and resumes, fiercely again; "Sir, your friend is the victim of an extraordinary resemblance, which is so much more painful to us than we could have made it to him that I have to struggle with my reason to believe that the apology should not come from his side rather than mine. He may feel that we have outraged him, but every look of his, every movement, every tone of his voice, is a mortal wound, a deadly insult to us. He should not live, sir, in the same solar system!" The General deals the floor another stab with his cane, while his eyes burn vindictively upon the mild brown orbs of Cummings, wide open with astonishment. He falters, with returning consciousness of his attitude : "I—I beg your pardon, sir; I am ridiculous." He closes his lips pathetically, and lets fall his head. When he lifts it again, it is to address Cummings with a singular gentleness : "I know that I speak to a gentleman."

Cummings.—"I try to be a good man."

General Wyatt.—"I had formed that idea of you, sir, in the pulpit. Will you do me the great kindness to answer a question, personal to myself, which I must ask?"

Cummings.—"By all means."

General Wyatt.—"You spoke of supposing me still in Paris. Are you aware of any circumstances—painful circumstances—connected with my presence there? Pardon my asking; I wouldn't press you if I could help."

Cummings, with reluctance.—"I had just heard something about—a letter from a friend"—

General Wyatt, bitterly.—"The news has travelled fast. Well, sir, a curious chance—a pitiless caprice of destiny—connects your friend with that miserable story." At Cummings's look of amaze: "Through no fault of his, sir j through no fault of his. Sir, I shall not seem to obtrude my trouble unjustifiably upon you when I tell you how; you will see that it was necessary for me to speak. I am glad you already know something of the affair, and I am sure that you will regard what I have to say with the right feeling of a gentleman,—of, as you say, a good man."

Cummings.—"Whatever you think necessary to say to me shall be sacred. But I hope you won't feel that it is necessary to say anything more. I am confident that when my friend has your assurance from me that what has happened is the result of a distressing association"—

General Wyatt.—"I thank you, sir. But something more is due to him; how much more you shall judge. Something more is due to us : I wish to preserve the appearance of sanity, in his eyes and your own. Nevertheless "—the Genera's tone and bearing perceptibly stiffen—"if you are reluctant"—

Cummings, with reverent cordiality.—"General Wyatt, I shall feel deeply honoured by whatever confidence you repose in me. I need not say how dear your fame is to us all." General Wyatt, visibly moved, bows to the young minister. "It was only on your account that I hesitated."

General Wyatt,—"Thanks. I understand. I will be explicit, but I will try to be brief. Your friend bears this striking, this painful resemblance to the man who has brought this blight upon us all; yes, sir,"—at Cummings's look of deprecation,—"to a scoundrel whom I hardly know how to characterise aright—in the presence of a clergyman, Two years ago—doubtless your correspondent has written—my wife and daughter (they were then abroad without me) met him in Paris; and he won the poor child's affection. My wife's judgment was also swayed in his favour,—against her first impulse of distrust; but when I saw him, I could not endure him. Yet I was helpless : my girl's happiness was bound up in him; all that I could do was to insist upon delay. He was an American, well related, unobjectionable by all the tests which society can apply, and I might have had to wait long for the proofs that an accident gave me against him. The man's whole soul was rotten; at the time he had wound himself into my poor girl's innocent heart, a woman was living who had the just and perhaps the legal claim of a wife upon him; he was a felon besides,—a felon shielded through pity for his friends by the man whose name he had forged; he was of course a liar and a coward : I beat him with my stick, sir. Ah! I made him confess his infamy under his own hand, and then "—the General advances defiantly upon Cummings, who unconsciously retires a pace—"and then I compelled him to break with my daughter. Do you think I did right?"

Cummings.—"I don't exactly understand."

General Wyatt.—"Why, sir, it happens often enough in this shabby world that a man gains a poor girl's love, and then jilts her. I chose what I thought the less terrible sorrow for my child. I could not tell her how filthily unworthy he was without bringing to her pure heart a sense of intolerable contamination; I could not endure to speak of it even to my wife. It seemed better that they should both suffer such wrong as a broken engagement might bring them than that they should know what I knew. He was master of the part, and played it well; he showed himself to them simply a heartless scoundrel, and he remains in my power, an outcast now and a convict whenever I will. My story, as it seems to be, is well known in Paris; but the worst is unknown. I choose still that it shall be thought my girl was the victim of a dastardly slight, and I bear with her and her mother the insolent pity with which the world visits such sorrow." He pauses, and then brokenly resumes : "The affair has not turned out as I hoped, in the little I could hope from it. My trust that the blow, which must sink so deeply into her heart, would touch her pride, and that this would help her to react against it, was mistaken. In such things it appears a woman has no pride; I did not know it; we men are different. The blow crushed her; that was all. Sometimes I am afraid that I must yet try the effect of the whole truth upon her; that I must try if the knowledge of all his baseness cannot restore to her the self-respect which the wrong done herself seems to have robbed her of. And yet I tremble lest the sense of his fouler shame—I may be fatally temporising; but in her present state, I dread any new shock for her; it may be death—I"—He pauses again, and sets his lips firmly; all at once he breaks into a sob. "I—I beg your pardon, sir."

Cummings.—"Don't! You wrong yourself and me. I have seen Miss Wyatt; but I hope"—

General Wyatt.—"You have seen her ghost. You have not seen the radiant creature that was once alive. Well, sir; enough of this. There is little left to trouble you with. We landed eight days ago, and I have since been looking about for some place in which my daughter could hide herself; I can't otherwise suggest her morbid sensitiveness, her terror of people. This region was highly commended to me for its healthfulness; but I have come upon this house by chance. I understood that it was empty, and I thought it more than probable that we might pass the autumn months here unmolested by the presence of any one belonging to our world, if not in entire seclusion. At the best, my daughter would hardly have been able to endure another change at once; so far as anything could give her pleasure, the beauty and the wild quiet of the region had pleased her, but she is now quite prostrated, sir,"—

Cummings, definitively.—"My friend will go away at once. There is nothing else for it."

General Wyatt.—"That is too much to ask."

Cummings.—"I won't conceal my belief that he will think so. But there can be no question with him when"—

General Wyatt.—"When you tell him our story?" After a moment: "Yes, he has a right to know it—as the rest of the world knows it. You must tell him, sir."

Cummings, gently.—"No, he need know nothing beyond the fact of this resemblance to some one painfully associated with your past lives. He is a man whose real tenderness of heart would revolt from knowledge that could inflict further sorrow upon you."

General Wyatt.—"Sir, will you convey to this friend of yours an old man's very humble apology, and sincere prayer for his forgiveness?"

Cummings.—"He will not exact anything of that sort. The evidence of misunderstanding will be clear to him at a word from me."

General Wyatt.—"But he has a right to this explanation from my own lips, and—Sir, I am culpably weak. But now that I have missed seeing him here, I confess that I would willingly avoid meeting him. The mere sound of his voice, as I heard it before I saw him, in first coming upon you, was enough to madden me. Can you excuse my senseless dereliction to him?"

Cummings.—"I will answer for him"

General Wyatt.—"Thanks. It seems monstrous that I should be asking and accepting these great favours. But you are doing a deed of charity to a helpless man utterly beggared in pride. He chokes with emotion, and does not speak for a moment, "Your friend is also—he is not also—a clergyman?"

Cummings, smiling.—"No. He is a painter."

General Wyatt.—"Is he a man of note? Successful in his profession?"

Cummings.—"Not yet. But that is certain to come."

General Wyatt.—"He is poor?"

Cummings.—"He is a young painter."

General Wyatt.—"Sir, excuse me. Had he planned to remain here some time yet?"

Cummings, reluctantly.—"He has been sketching here. He had expected to stay through October."

General Wyatt.—"You make the sacrifice hard to accept—I beg your pardon! But I must accept it. I am bound hand and foot."

Cummings.—"I am sorry to have been obliged to tell you this."

General Wyatt.—"I obliged you, sir; I obliged you. Give me your advice, sir; you know your friend. What shall I do? I am not rich. I don't belong to a branch of the government service in which people enrich themselves. But I have my pay; and if your friend could sell me the pictures he's been painting here"—

Cummings.—"That's quite impossible. There is no form in which I could propose such a thing to a man of his generous pride."

General Wyatt.—"Well, then, sir, I must satisfy myself as I can to remain his debtor. Will you kindly undertake to tell him?"

An Elderly Serving-Woman, who appears timidly and anxiously at the right-hand door.—"General Wyatt."

General Wyatt, with a start.—"Yes, Mary! Well?"

Mary, in vanishing.—"Mrs, Wyatt wishes to speak with you."

General Wyatt, going up to Cummings.—"I must go, sir. I leave unsaid what I cannot even try to say." He offers his hand.

Cummings, grasping the proffered hand.—

"Everything is understood." But as Mr. Cummings returns from following General Wyatt to the door, his face does not confirm the entire security of his words. He looks anxious and perturbed, and when he has taken up his hat and stick, he stands pondering absent-mindedly. At last he puts on his hat and starts briskly toward the door. Before he reaches it, he encounters Bartlett, who advances abruptly into the room. "Oh! I was going to look for you."

VI.
CUMMINGS and BARTLETT.

Bartlett, sulkily.—"Were you?" He walks, without looking at Cummings, to where his painter's paraphernalia are lying, and begins to pick them up.

Cummings.—"Yes." In great embarrassment: "Bartlett, General Wyatt has been here."

Bartlett, without looking round.—"Who is General Wyatt?"

Cummings.—"I mean the gentleman who—whom you wouldn't wait to see."

Bartlett.—"Um!" He has gathered the things into his arms, and is about to leave the room.

Cummings, in great distress.—"Bartlett, Bartlett! Don't go! I implore you, if you have any regard for me whatever, to hear what I have to say. It's boyish, it's cruel, it's cowardly to behave as you're doing!"

Bartlett.—"Anything more, Mr. Cummings? I give you benefit of clergy."

Cummings.—"I take it—to denounce your proceeding as something that you'll always be sorry for and ashamed of."

Bartlett.—"Oh! Then, if you have quite freed your mind, I think I may go."

Cummings.—"No, no! You mustn't go. Don't go, my dear fellow. Forgive me! I know how insulted you feel, but upon my soul it's all a mistake,—it is, indeed. General Wyatt"—Bartlett falters a moment and stands as if irresolute whether to stay and listen or push on out of the room—"the young lady—I don't know how to begin!"

Bartlett, relenting a little.—"Well? I'm sorry for you, Cummings. I left a very awkward business to you, and it wasn't yours either. As for General Wyatt, as he chooses to call himself"—

Cummings, in amaze.—"Call himself? It's his name!"

Bartlett—"Oh, very likely! So is King David his name, when he happens to be in a Scriptural craze. What explanation have you been commissioned to make me? What apology?"

Cummings.—"The most definite, the most satisfactory. You resemble in a most extraordinary manner a man who has inflicted an abominable wrong upon these people, a treacherous and cowardly villain"—

Bartlett, in a burst of fury.—"Stop! Is that your idea of an apology, an explanation? Isn't it enough that I should be threatened, and vilified, and have people fainting at the sight of me, but I must be told by way of reparation that it all happens because I look like a rascal?"

Cummings.—"My dear friend! Do listen to me!"

Bartlett.—"No, sir, I won't listen to you! I've listened too much! What right, I should like to know, have they to find this resemblance in me? And do they suppose that I'm going to be placated by being told that they treat me like a rogue because I look like one? It's a little too much A man calls 'Stop thief' after me and expects me to be delighted when he tells me I look like a thief! The reparation is an additional insult. I don't choose to know that they fancy this infamous resemblance in me. Their pretending it is an outrage; and your reporting it to me is an offence. Will you tell them what I say? Will you tell this General Wyatt and the rest of his Bedlam-broke-loose, that they may all go to the"—

Cummings.—"For shame, for shame! You outrage a terrible sorrow! You insult a trouble sore to death! You trample upon an anguish that should be sacred to your tears!"

Bartlett, resting his elbow on the corner of the piano.—"What—what do you mean, Cummings?"

Cummings.—"What do I mean? What you are not worthy to know! I mean that these people, against whom you vent your stupid rage, are worthy of angelic pity. I mean that by some disastrous mischance you resemble to the life, in tone, manner, and feature, the wretch who won that poor girl's heart, and then crushed it; who—Bartlett, look here! These are the people—this is the young lady—of whom my friend wrote me from Paris : do you understand?"

Bartlett, in a dull bewilderment,—"No, I don't understand."

Cummings.—"Why, you know what we were talking of just before they came in : you know what I told you of that cruel business."

Bartlett.—"Well?"

Cummings.—"Well, this is the young lady"—

Bartlett, dauntedly.—"Oh, come now! You don't expect me to believe that! It isn't a stage-play,"

Cummings.—"Indeed, indeed, I tell you the miserable truth."

Bartlett.—"Do you mean to say that this is the young girl who was jilted in that way? Who—Do you mean—Do you intend to tell me—Do you suppose—Cummings"—

Cummings.—"Yes, yes, yes!"

Bartlett.—"Why, man, she's in Paris, according to your own showing!"

Cummings.—"She was in Paris three weeks ago. They have just brought her home, to help her hide her suffering, as if it were her shame, from all who know it. They are in this house by chance, but they are here. I mean what I say. You must believe it, shocking and wild as it is."

Bartlett, after a prolonged silence in which he seems trying to realise the fact.—"If you were a man capable of such a ghastly joke—but that's impossible." He is silent again, as before. "And I—What did you say about me? That I look like a man who"—He stops and stares into Cummings's face without speaking, as if he were trying to puzzle the mystery out; then, with fallen head, he muses in a voice of devout and reverent tenderness : "That—that—broken—lily! Oh!" With a sudden start he flings his burden upon the closed piano, whose hidden strings hum with the blow, and advances upon Cummings: "And you can tell it? Shame on you! It ought to be known to no one upon earth! And you—you show that gentle creature's death-wound to teach something like human reason to a surly dog like me? Oh, it's monstrous! I wasn't worth it. Better have let me go, where I would, how I would. What did it matter what I thought or said? And I—I look like that devil, do I? I have his voice, his face, his movement? Cummings, you've over-avenged yourself."

Cummings.—"Don't take it that way, Bartlett. It is hideous. But I didn't make it so, nor you. It's a fatality, it's a hateful chance. But you see now, don't you, Bartlett, how the sight of you must affect them, and how anxious her father must be to avoid you? He most humbly asked your forgiveness, and he hardly knew how to ask that you would not let her see you again. But I told him there could be no question with you; that of course you would prevent it, and at once. I know it's a great sacrifice to expect you to go"—

Bartlett.—"Go? What are you talking about?" He breaks again from the daze into which he had relapsed. "If there's a hole on the face of the earth where I can hide myself from them, I want to find it. What do you think I'm made of? Go? I ought to be shot away out of a mortar; I ought to be struck away by lightning! Oh, I can't excuse you, Cummings! The indelicacy, the brutality of telling me that! No, no,—I can't overlook it." He shakes his head and walks away from his friend; then he returns, and bends on him a look of curious inquiry. "Am I really such a ruffian"—he speaks very gently, almost meekly, now—"that you didn't believe anything short of that would bring me to my senses? Who told you this of her?"

Cummings.—"Her father."

Bartlett.—"Oh, that's too loathsome! Had the man no soul, no mercy? Did he think me such a consummate beast that nothing less would drive me away? Yes, he did! Yes, I made him think so! Oh!" He hangs his head and walks away with a shudder.

Cummings.—"I don't know that he did you that injustice; but I'm afraid I did. I was at my wits' end."

Bartlett, very humbly.—"Oh, I don't know that you were wrong."

Cummings.—"I suppose that his anxiety for her life made it comparatively easy for him to speak of the hurt to her pride. She can't be long for this world."

Bartlett.—"No, she had the dying look!" After a long pause, in which he has continued to wander aimlessly about the room: "Cummings, is it necessary that you should tell him you told me?"

Cummings.—"You know I hate concealments of any kind, Bartlett."

Bartlett.—"Oh, well; do it then!"

Cummings.—"But I don't know that we shall see him again; and even if we do, I don't see how I can tell him unless he asks. It's rather painful."

Bartlett.—"Well, take that little sin on your conscience if you can. It seems to me too ghastly that I should know what you've told me; it's indecent. Cummings,"—after another pause,—"how does a man go about such a thing? How does he contrive to tell the woman whose heart he has won that he doesn't care for her, and break the faith that she would have staked her life on? Oh, I know,—women do such things, too; but it's different, by a whole world's difference. A man comes and a man goes, but a woman stays. The world is before him after that happens, and we don't think him much of a man if he can't get over it. But she, she has been sought out; she has been made to believe that her smile and her looks are heaven, poor, foolish, helpless idol! her fears have been laid, all her pretty maidenly traditions, her proud reserves overcome; she takes him into her inmost soul,—to find that his love is a lie, a lie! Imagine it! She can't do anything. She can't speak. She can't move as long as she lives. She must stay where she has been left, and look and act as if nothing had happened. Oh, good Heaven! And I, I look like a man who could do that!" After a silence : "I feel as if there were blood on me!" He goes to the piano, and gathering up his things turns about towards Cummings again: "Come, man; I'm going. It's sacrilege to stay an instant,—to exist."

Cummings.—"Don't take it in that way, Bartlett. I blame myself very much for not having spared you in what I said. I wouldn't have told you of it, if I could have supposed that an accidental resemblance of the sort would distress you so."

Bartlett, contritely.—"You had to tell me. I forced you to extreme measures. I'm quite worthy to look like him. Good Lord! I suppose I should be capable of his work." He moves towards the door with his burden, but before he reaches it General Wyatt, from the corridor, meets him with an air of confused agitation. Bartlett halts awkwardly, and some of the things slip from his hold to the floor.

VII.
GENERAL WYATT, CUMMINGS, and BARTLETT.

General Wyatt—"Sir, I am glad to see you." He pronounces the civility with a manner evidently affected by the effort to reconcile Bartlett's offensive personal appearance with his own sense of duty. "I—I was sorry to miss you before; and now I wish—Your friend"—referring with an inquiring glance to Cummings—"has explained to you the cause of our very extraordinary behaviour, and I hope you"—

Bartlett.—"Mr. Cummings has told me that I have the misfortune to resemble some one with whom you have painful associations. That is quite enough, and entirely justifies you. I am going at once, and I trust you will forgive my rudeness in absenting myself a moment ago. I have a bad temper; but I never could forgive myself if I had forced my friend "—he turns and glares warningly at Cummings, who makes a faint pantomime of conscientious protest as Bartlett proceeds—"to hear anything more than the mere fact from you. No, no,"—as General Wyatt seems about to speak,—"it would be atrocious in me to seek to go behind it. I wish to know nothing more." Cummings gives signs of extreme unrest at being made a party to this tacit deception, and General Wyatt, striking his palms hopelessly together, walks to the other end of the room. Bartlett touches the fallen camp-stool with his foot. "Cummings, will you be kind enough to put that on top of this other rubbish? " He indicates his armful, and as Cummings complies, he says in a swift fierce whisper: "Her secret is mine. If you dare to hint that you've told it to me, I'll—I'll assault you in your own pulpit." Then to General Wyatt, who is returning toward him : "Good-morning, sir."

General Wyatt—"Oh! Ah! Stop! That is, don't go! Really, sir, I don't know what to say. I must have seemed to you like a madman a moment ago, and now

I've come to play the fool." Bartlett and Cummings look their surprise, and General Wyatt hurries on: "I asked your friend to beg you to go away, and now I am here to beg you to remain. It's perfectly ridiculous, sir, I know, and I can say nothing in defence of the monstrous liberties I have taken. Sir, the matter is simply this: my daughter's health is so frail that her life seems to hang by a thread, and I am powerless to do anything against her wish. It may be a culpable weakness, but I cannot help it. When I went back to her from seeing your friend, she immediately divined what my mission had been, and it had the contrary effect from what I had expected. Well, sir! Nothing would content her but that I should return and ask you to stay. She looks upon it as the sole reparation we can make you."

Bartlett, gently.—"I understand that perfectly; and may I beg you to say that in going away I thanked her with all my heart, and ventured to leave her my best wishes?" He bows as if to go.

General Wyatt, detaining him.—"Excuse me—thanks—but—but I am afraid she will not be satisfied with that. She will be satisfied with nothing less than your remaining. It is the whim of a sick child—which I must ask you to indulge. In a few days, sir, I hope we may be able to continue on our way. It would be simply unbearable pain to her to know that we had driven you away, and you must stay to show that you have forgiven the wrong we have done you.'

Bartlett—"That's nothing, less than nothing. But I was thinking—I don't care for myself in the matter—that Miss Wyatt is proposing a very unnecessary annoyance for you all. My friend can remain and assure her that I have no feeling whatever about the matter, and in the meantime I can remove—the embarrassment—of my presence."

General Wyatt—"Sir, you are very considerate, very kind. My own judgment is in favour of your course, and yet"—

Cummings.—"I think my friend is right, and that when he is gone"—

General Wyatt.—"Well, sir! well, sir! It may be the best way. I think it is the best. We will venture upon it. Sir,"—to Bartlett,—"may I have the honour of taking your hand?" Bartlett lays down his burden on the piano, and gives his hand. "Thank you, thank you! You will not regret this goodness. God bless you! May you always prosper!"

Bartlett—"Good-bye; and say to Miss Wyatt"—At these words he pauses, arrested by an incomprehensible dismay in General Wyatt's face, and turning about he sees Cummings transfixed at the apparition of Miss Wyatt advancing directly toward himself, while her mother coming behind her exchanges signals of helplessness and despair with the General. The young girl's hair, thick and bronze, has been heaped in hasty but beautiful masses on her delicate head; as she stands with fallen eyes before Bartlett, the heavy lashes lie dark on her pale cheeks, and the blue of her eyes shows through their transparent lids. She has a fan with which she makes a weak pretence of playing, and which she puts to her lips as if to hide the low murmur that escapes from them as she raises her eyes to Bartlett's face.

VIII.
CONSTANCE, MRS. WYATT, and the others.

Constance, with a phantom-like effort at hauteur.—"I hope you have been able to forgive the annoyance we caused you, and that you won't let it drive you away." She lifts her eyes with a slow effort, and starts with a little gasp as they fall upon his face, and then remains trembling before him while he speaks.

Bartlett, reverently.—"I am to do whatever you wish. I have no annoyance—but the fear that—that"—

Constance, in a husky whisper.—"Thanks!" As she turns from him to go back to her mother, she moves so frailly that he involuntarily puts out his hand.

Mrs. Wyatt, starting forward.—"No!" But Constance clutches his extended arm with one of her pale hands, and staying herself for a moment lifts her eyes again to his, looks steadily at him with her face half turned upon him, and then, making a slight, sidelong inclination of the head, releases his arm and goes to her mother, who supports her to one of the easy-chairs and kneels beside her when she sinks into it. Bartlett, after an instant of hesitation, bows silently and withdraws, Cummings having already vanished, Constance watches him going, and then hides her face on her mother's neck.

II.
DISTINCTIONS AND DIFFERENCES.

I.
CONSTANCE and MRS. WYATT.

Constance.—"And he is still here? He is going to stay on, mother?" She reclines in a low folding chair, and languidly rests her head against one of the pillows with which her mother has propped her; on the bright coloured shawl which has been thrown over her lie her pale hands loosely holding her shut fan. Her mother stands half across the parlour from her, and wistfully surveys her work, to see if some touch may not yet be added for the girl's comfort.

Mrs. Wyatt—"Yes, my child. He will stay. He told your father he would stay."

Constance.—"That's very kind of him. He's very good."

Mrs. Wyatt, seating herself before her daughter.—"Do you really wish him to stay? Remember how weak you are, Constance. If you are taking anything upon yourself out of a mistaken sense of duty, of compunction, you are not kind to your poor father or to me. Not that I mean to reproach you."

Constance.—"Oh, no. And I am not unkind to you in the way you think. I'm selfish enough in wishing him to stay. I can't help wanting to see him again and again,—it's so strange, so strange. All this past week, whenever I've caught a glimpse of him, it's been like an apparition; and whenever he has spoken, it has been like a ghost speaking. But I haven't been afraid since the first time. No, there's been a dreary comfort in it; you won't understand it; I can't understand it myself; but I know now why people are glad to see their dead in dreams. If the ghost went, there would be nothing."

Mrs. Wyatt.—"Constance, you break my heart!"

Constance.—"Yes, I know it; it's because I've none." She remains a little space without speaking, while she softly fingers the edges of the fan lying in her lap. "I suppose we shall become more acquainted, if he stays?"

Mrs. Wyatt.—"Why, not necessarily, dear. You need know nothing more of him than you do now. He seems very busy, and not in the least inclined to intrude upon us. Your father thinks him a little odd, but very gentlemanly."

Constance, dreamily.—"I wonder what he would think if he knew that the man whom I would have given my life did not find my love worth having? I suppose it was worthless; but it seemed so much in the giving; it was that deceived me. He was wiser. Oh, me!" After a silence : "Mother, why was I so different from other girls?"

Mrs. Wyatt.—"So different, Constance? You were only different in being lovelier and better than others."

Constance.—"Ah, that's the mistake! If that were true, it could never have happened. Other girls, the poorest and plainest, are kept faith with; but I was left. There must have been something about me that made him despise me. Was I silly, mother? Was I too bold, too glad to have him care for me? I was so happy that I couldn't help showing it. May be that displeased him. I must have been dull and tiresome. And I suppose I was somehow repulsive, and at last he couldn't bear it any longer and had to break with me. Did I dress queerly? I know I looked ridiculous at times; and people laughed at me before him."

Mrs. Wyatt.—"Oh, Constance, Constance! Can't you understand that it was his un-worthiness alone, his wicked heartlessness?"

Constance, with gentle slowness.—"No, I can't understand that. It happened after we had learned to know each other so well If he had been fickle, it would have happened long before that. It was something odious in me that he didn't see at first. I have thought it out. It seems strange now that people could ever have tolerated me." Desolately: "Well, they have their revenge."

Mrs. Wyatt.—"Their revenge on you, Constance? What harm did you ever do them, my poor child? Oh, you mustn't let these morbid fancies overcome you. Where is our Constance that used to be,—our brave, bright girl, that nothing could daunt, and nothing could sadden?"

Constance, sobbing.—"Dead, dead!"

Mrs. Wyatt—"I can't understand! You are so young still, and with the world all before you. Why will you let one man's baseness blacken it all, and blight your young life so? Where is your pride, Constance?"

Constance.—"Pride? What have I to do with pride? A thing like me!"

Mrs. Wyatt.—"Oh, child, you're pitiless! It seems as if you took a dreadful pleasure in torturing those who love you."

Constance.—"You've said it, mother. I do. I know now that I am a vampire, and that it's my hideous fate to prey upon those who are dearest to me. He must have known, he must have felt the vampire in me."

Mrs. Wyatt,—"Constance!"

Constance.—"But at least I can be kind to those who care nothing for me. Who is this stranger? He must be an odd kind of man to forgive us. What is he, mother?— if he is anything in himself; he seems to me only a likeness, not a reality."

Mrs. Wyatt—"He is a painter, your father says." Mrs. Wyatt gives a quick sigh of relief, and makes haste to confirm the direction of the talk away from Constance : "He is painting some landscapes here. That friend of his who went to-day is a cousin of your father's old friend, Major Cummings. He's a minister."

Constance.—"What is the painter's name? Not that it matters. But I must call him something if I meet him again."

Mrs. Wyatt.—"Mr. Bartlett."

Constance.—"Oh yes, I forgot." She falls into a brooding silence. "I wonder if he will despise me—if he will be like in that too?" Mrs. Wyatt sighs patiently. "Why do you mind what I say, mother? I'm not worth it. I must talk on, or else go mad with the mystery of what has been. We were so happy; he was so good to me, so kind; there was nothing but papa's not seeming to like him; and then suddenly, in an instant, he turns and strikes me down! Yes, it was like a deadly blow. If you don't let me believe that it was because he saw all at once that I was utterly unworthy, I can't believe in anything."

Mrs. Wyatt—"Hush, Constance; you don't know what you're saying."

Constance.—"Oh, I know too well! And now this stranger, who is so like him— who has all his looks, who has his walk, who has his voice,—won't he have his insight too? I had better show myself for what I am, at once—weak, stupid, selfish, false; it'll save me the pain of being found out. Pain? Oh, I'm past hurting! Why do you cry, mother? I'm not worth your tears."

Mrs, Wyatt.—"You're all the world to us, Constance; you know it, child. Your poor father"—

Constance.—"Does papa really like me?"

Mrs. Wyatt..—"Constance!"

Constance.—"No; but why should he? He never liked him; and sometimes I've wondered, if it wasn't papa's not liking him that first set him against me. Of course, it was best he should find me out, but still I can't keep from thinking that if he had never begun to dislike me! I noticed from the first that after papa had been with us he was cold and constrained. Mother, I had better say it : I don't believe I love papa as I ought. There's something in my heart—some hardness—against him when he's kindest to me. If he had only been kinder to him"—

Mrs. Wyatt.—"Kinder to him? Constance, you drive me wild! Kind to a wolf, kind to a snake! Kind to the thief who has robbed us of all that made our lives dear; who stole your love, and then your hope, your health, your joy, your pride, your peace! And you think your father might have been kinder to him! Constance, you were our little girl when the war began,—the last of brothers and sisters that had died. You seemed given to our later years to console and comfort us for those that had been taken; and you were so bright and gay! All through those dreadful days and months and years you were our stay and hope,—mine at home, his in the field. Our letters were full of you,—like young people's with their first child; all that you did and said I had to tell him, and then he had to talk it over in his answers back. When he came home at last after the peace—can you remember it, Constance?"

Constance.—"I can remember a little girl that ran down the street, and met an officer on horseback. He was all tanned and weather-beaten; he sat his horse at the head of his troop like a statue of bronze. When he saw her come running, dancing down the street, he leaped from his horse and caught her in his arms, and hugged her close and kissed her, and set her all crying and laughing in his saddle, and walked on beside her; and the men burst out with a wild yell, and the ragged flags flapped over her, and the music flashed out"—She rises in her chair with the thrill of her recollection; her voice comes free and full, and her pale cheeks flush; suddenly she sinks back upon the pillows : "Was it really I, mother?"

Mrs. Wyatt.—"Yes, it was you, Constance. And do you remember all through your school-days, how proud and fond he was of you? what presents and feasts and pleasures he was always making you? I thought he would spoil you; he took you everywhere with him, and wanted to give you everything. When I saw you growing up with his pride and quick temper, I trembled, but I felt safe when I saw that you had his true and tender heart too. You can never know what a pang it cost him to part with you when we went abroad, but you can't forget how he met you in Paris?"

Constance.—"Oh, no, no! Poor papa!"

Mrs. Wyatt—"Oh, child! And I could tell you something of his bitter despair when he saw the man"—

Constance, wearily.—"You needn't tell me. I knew it as soon as they met, without looking at either of them."

Mrs. Wyatt—"And when the worst that he feared came true, he was almost glad, I believe. He thought, and I thought, that your self-respect would come to your aid against such treachery."

Constance.—"My self-respect? Now I know you've not been talking of me."

Mrs. Wyatt, desperately.—"Oh, what shall I do?"

Mary, the serving-woman, at the door.—"If you please, Mrs. Wyatt, I can't open Miss Constance's hat-box."

Mrs. Wyatt, rising.—"Oh, yes. There's something the matter with the lock. I'll come, Mary." She looks at Constance.

Constance.—"Yes, go, mother. I'm perfectly well here. I like being alone well enough." As Mrs. Wyatt, after a moment's reluctance, goes out, the girl's heavy eyelids fall, and she lies motionless against her pillows, while the fan, released from her careless hold, slides slowly over the shawl, and drops with a light clash upon the floor. She starts at the sound, and utters a little involuntary cry at sight of Bartlett, who stands irresolute in the doorway on her right. He makes as if to retreat, but at a glance from her he remains.

II.
BARTLETT and CONSTANCE,

Bartlett, with a sort of subdued gruffness.—"I'm afraid I disturbed you*"

Constance, passively.—"No, I think it was my fan. It fell."

Bartlett.—"I'm glad I can lay the blame on the fan." He comes abruptly forward and picks it up for her. She makes no motion to receive it, and he lays it on her lap.

Constance, starting from the abstraction in which she has been gazing at him.—"Oh! thanks."

Bartlett, with constraint,—"I hope you're better this morning?"

Constance.—"Yes." She has again fallen into a dreamy study of him, as unconscious, apparently, as if he were a picture before her, the effect of which is to reduce him to a state of immovable awkwardness. At last he tears himself loose from the spot on which he has been petrifying, and takes refuge in the business which has brought him into the room.

Bartlett.—"I came to look for one of my brushes. It must have dropped out of my traps here the other day." He goes up to the piano and looks about the floor, while Constance's gaze follows him in every attitude and movement. "Ah, here it is! I knew it would escape the broom under the landlady's relaxed regime. If you happen to drop anything in this room, Miss Wyatt, you needn't be troubled; you can always find it just where it fell." Miss Wyatt's fan again slips to the floor, and Bartlett again picks it up and restores it to her : "A case in point."

Constance, blushing faintly.—"Don't do it for me. It isn't worth while."

Bartlett, gravely.—"It doesn't take a great deal of time, and the exercise does me good." Constance faintly smiles, but does not relax her vigilance. "Isn't that light rather strong for you?" He goes to the glass doors opening on the balcony, and offers to draw down one of their shades.

Constance.—"It doesn't make any difference."

Bartlett, bluffly.—"If it's disagreeable it makes some difference. Is it disagreeable?"

Constance.—"The light's strong"—Bartlett dashes the curtain down—"but I could see the mountain." He pulls the curtain up.

Bartlett.—"I beg your pardon." He again falls into statue-like discomposure under Miss Wyatt's gaze, which does not seek the distant slopes of Ponkwasset, in spite of the lifted curtain.

Constance.—"What is the name? Do you know?"

Bartlett—" Whose? Oh! Ponkwasset. It's not a pretty name, but it's aboriginal. And it doesn't hurt the mountain." Recovering a partial volition, he shows signs of a purpose to escape, when Miss Wyatt's next question arrests him.

Constance.—"Are you painting it, Mr.—Bartlett?"

Bartlett, with a laugh.—"Oh no, I don't soar so high as mountains; I only lift my eyes to a tree here and there, and a bit of pasture and a few of the lowlier and friendlier sort of rocks." He now so far effects his purpose as to transfer his unwieldy presence to a lateral position as regards Miss Wyatt. The girl mechanically turns her head upon the pillow and again fixes her sad eyes upon him.

Constance.—"Have you ever been up it?"

Bartlett.—"Yes, half a dozen times."

Constance.—"Is it hard to climb—like the Swiss mountains?"

Bartlett—"You must speak for the Swiss mountains after you've tried Ponkwasset, Miss Wyatt. I've never been abroad."

Constance, her large eyes dilating with surprise.—"Never been abroad?"

Bartlett.—"I enjoy that distinction."

Constance.—"Oh! I thought you had been abroad." She speaks with a slow, absent, earnest accent, regarding him, as always, with a look of wistful bewilderment.

Bartlett, struggling uneasily for his habitual lightness.—"I'm sorry to disappoint you, Miss Wyatt. I will go abroad as soon as possible. I'm going out in a boat this morning to work at a bit on the point of the island yonder, and I'll take lessons in seafaring." Bartlett, managing at last to get fairly behind Miss Wyatt's chair, indulges himself in a long, low sigh of relief, and taking out his handkerchief rubs his face with it.

Constance, with sudden, meek compunction.—" I've been detaining you."

Bartlett, politely coming forward again.—"Oh no, not at all! I m afraid I've tired you."

Constance.—"No, I'm glad to have you stay." In the unconscious movement necessary to follow Bartlett in his changes of position, the young girl has loosened one of the pillows that prop her head. It slowly disengages itself and drops to the floor. Bartlett, who has been crushing his brush against the ball of his thumb, gives a start of terror, and looks from Constance to the pillow, and back again to Constance in despair.

Constance.—"Never mind." She tries to adjust her head to the remaining pillows, and then desists in evident discomfort.

Bartlett, in great agony of spirit.—"I—I'm afraid you miss it."

Constance.—"Oh no."

Bartlett.—"Shall I call your mother, Miss Wyatt?"

Constance.—"No. Oh no. She will be here presently. Thank you so much." Bartlett eyes the pillow in renewed desperation.

Bartlett.—"Do you think—do you suppose I could"—Recklessly; "Miss Wyatt, let me put back that pillow for you!"

Constance, promptly, with a little flush :—"Why, you're very good! I'm ashamed to trouble you." As she speaks, she raises her head, and lifts herself forward slightly by help of the chair-arms; two more pillows topple out, one on either side, unknown to her.

Bartlett, maddened by the fresh disaster:—"Good Lord!" He flings himself wildly upon the first pillow, and crams it into the chair behind Miss Wyatt; then without giving his courage time to flag, he seizes the others, and packs them in on top of it: "Will that do?" He stands hot and flushed, looking down upon her, as she makes a gentle attempt to adjust herself to the mass.

Constance.—"Oh, perfectly." She puts her hand behind her and feebly endeavours to modify Bartlett's arrangement.

Bartlett—"What is it?"

Constance.—"Oh—nothing. Ah—would—would you draw this one a little—

toward you? So! Thanks. And that one—out a little on the—other side? You're very kind; that's right. And this one under my neck—lift it up a little? Ah, thank you ever so much." Bartlett, in a fine frenzy, obeying these instructions, Miss Wyatt at last reposes herself against the pillows, looks up into his embarrassed face, and deeply blushes; then she turns suddenly white, and weakly catching up her fan she passes it once or twice before her face, and lets it fall: "I'm a little—faint." Bartlett seizes the fan, and after a moment of silent self-dedication kneels down beside her chair, and fans her.

Constance, after a moment:—"Thanks, thanks. You are very good. I'm better now. I'm ashamed to have troubled you. But I seem to live only to give trouble."

Bartlett, with sudden deep tenderness :—"Oh, Miss Wyatt, you mustn't say that. I'm sure I—we all—that is—shall I call your mother now, Miss Wyatt?"

Constance, after a deep breath, firmly:—"No, I'm quite well, now. She is busy. But I know I'm keeping you from your work,"—with ever so slight a wan little smile. "I mustn't do that."

Bartlett.—"Oh, you're not keeping me! There's no hurry. I can work later just as well."

Constance.—   "Then,"—with a glance at his devout posture, of which Bartlett has himself become quite unconscious,—"won't you sit down, Mr. Bartlett?"

Bartlett, restored to consciousness and confusion :—"Thanks; I think it will be better." He rises, and in his embarrassment draws a chair to the spot on which he has been kneeling, and sits down very close to her. He keeps the fan in his hand, as he talks: "It's rather nice out there, Miss Wyatt,—there on the island. You must be rowed out as soon as you can stand it. The General would like it."

Constance.—"Is it a large place, the island?"

Bartlett.—"About two acres, devoted exclusively to golden-rod and granite. The fact is, I was going to make a little study of golden-rod and granite, there. You shall visit the Fortunate Isle in my sketch, this afternoon, and see whether you'd like to go, really. People camp out there in the summer. Who knows, but if you keep on—gaining—this way, you may yet feel like camping out there yourself before you go away? You do begin to feel better, don't you? Everybody cries up this air."

Constance.—"It's very pleasant; it seems fine and pure. Is the island a pretty place?"

Bartlett, glancing out at it over his shoulder:—"Well, you get the best of it from the parlour window, here. Not that it's so bad when you're on it; there's a surly, frugal, hard-headed kind of beauty about it,—like the local human nature—and it has its advantages. If you were camping out there, you could almost provision yourself from the fish and wild fowl of the surrounding waters,—supposing any of your party liked to fish or shoot. Does your father like shooting?"

Constance.—"No, I don't believe he cares for it."

Bartlett.—"I'm glad of that. I shall be spared the painful hospitality of pointing out the best places for ducks." At an inquiring look from Constance: "I'm glad for their sakes, not mine; I don't want to kill them."

Constance, with grave mistrust:—"Not like shooting?"

Bartlett—"No, I think it's the sneak-ingest sort of assassination; it's the pleasure of murder without the guilt. If you must kill, you ought to be man enough to kill something that you'll suffer remorse for. Do you consider those atrocious sentiments, Miss Wyatt? I assure you that they're entirely my own."

Constance, blankly.—"I wasn't thinking—I was thinking—I supposed you liked shooting."

Bartlett, laughing uneasily.—"How did you get that impression?"

Constance, evasively.—"I thought all gentlemen did."

Bartlett—"They do in this region. It's the only thing that can comfort them in affliction. The other day our ostler's brother lost his sweetheart—she died, poor girl—and the ostler and another friend had him over here to cheer him up. They took him to the stable, and whittled round among the stalls with him half the forenoon, and let him rub down some of the horses; they stood him out among the vegetables and let him gather some of the new kind of potato-bugs; they made him sit in the office with his feet on top of the stove; they played billiards with him; but he showed no signs of resignation till they borrowed three squirrel-guns and started with him to the oak woods yonder. That seemed to 'fetch' him. You should have seen them trudging off together with their guns all aslant,—this way,—the stricken lover in the middle!" Bartlett rises to illustrate, and then at the deepening solemnity of Constance's face he desists in sudden dismay : " Miss Wyatt, I' ve shocked you!"

Constance.—"Oh, no—no!"

Bartlett.—"It was shocking. I wonder how I could do it! I—I thought it would amuse you."

Constance, mournfully.—"It did, thank you, very much." After a pause : " I didn't know you liked—joking."

Bartlett.—"Ah! I don't believe I do—all kinds. Good Lord—I beg your pardon." Bartlett turns away with an air of guilty consciousness, and goes to the window and looks out, Constance's gaze following him : "It's a wonderful day!" He comes back toward her : "What a pity you couldn't be carried there in your chair!"

Constance.—"I'm not equal to that yet." Presently : "Then you—like—nature?"

Bartlett.—"Why, that's mere shop in a landscape painter. I get my bread and butter by her. At least I ought to have some feeling of gratitude."

Constance, hastily.—"Of course, of course. It's very stupid of me, asking."

Bartlett, with the desperate intention of grappling with the situation.—"I see you have a passion for formulating, classifying people, Miss Wyatt. That's all very well, if one's characteristics were not so very characteristic of everybody else. But I generally find in my moments of self-consciousness, when I've gone round priding myself that such and such traits are my peculiar property, that the first man I meet has them all and as many more, and isn't the least proud of them. I dare say you don't see anything very strange in them, so far."

Constance, musingly.—"Oh, yes; very strange indeed. They're all—wrong!"

Bartlett.—"Well! I don't know—I'm very sorry—Then you consider it wrong not to like shooting and to be fond of joking and nature, and "—

Constance, bewilderedly.—"Wrong? Oh no!"

Bartlett.—"Oh, I'm glad to hear it. But you just said it was."

Constance, slowly recalling herself, with a painful blush, at last—"I meant—I meant I didn't expect any of those things of you."

Bartlett, with a smile.—"Well, on reflection, I don't know that I did, either. I think they must have come without being expected. Upon my word, I'm tempted to propose something very ridiculous."

Constance, uneasily.—"Yes? What is that?"

Bartlett.—"That you'll let me try to guess you out. I've failed so miserably in my own case, that I feel quite encouraged."

Constance, morbidly.—"I'm not worth the trouble of guessing out."

Bartlett.—"That means no. You always mean no by yes, because you can't bear to say no. That is the mark of a very deep and darkling nature. I feel that I could go on and read your mind perfectly, but I'm afraid to do it. Let's get back to myself. I can't allow that you've failed to read my mind aright; I think you were careless about it. Will you give your intuitions one more chance?"

Constance, with an anxious smile.—"Oh yes."

Bartlett—"All those traits and tastes which we both find so unexpected in me are minor matters at the most. The great test question remains. If you answer it rightly, you prove yourself a mind-reader of wonderful power; if you miss it—The question is simply this : Do I like smoking?"

Constance, instantly, with a quick, involuntary pressure of her handkerchief to her delicate nostrils.—"Oh, yes, indeed!"

Bartlett, daunted and reddening.—"Miss Wyatt, you have been deluding me. You are really a mind-reader of great subtlety."

Constance.—"I don't know—I can't say that it was mind-reading exactly." She lifts her eyes to his, and in his embarrassment he passes his hand over his forehead and then feels first in one pocket, and then in the other for his handkerchief; suddenly he twitches it forth, and with it a pipe, half a dozen cigars, and a pouch of smoking tobacco, which fly in different directions over the floor. As he stoops in dismay and sweeps together these treasures, she cries : "Oh, it didn't need all that to prove it!" and breaks into a wild, helpless laugh, and striving to recover herself with many little moans and sighs behind her handkerchief, laughs on and on: "Oh, don't! I oughtn't! Oh dear, oh dear!" When at last she lies spent with her reluctant mirth, and uncovers her face, Bartlett is gone, and it is her mother who stands over her, looking down at her with affectionate misgiving.

III.
MRS. WYATT and CONSTANCE.

Mrs. Wyatt.—"Laughing, Constance?"

Constance, with a burst of indignant tears.—"Yes, yes! Isn't it shocking? It's horrible! He made me."

Mrs. Wyatt.—"He?"

Constance, beginning to laugh again.—"Mr. Bartlett; he's been here. Oh, I wish I wouldn't be so silly!"

Mrs. Wyatt.—"Made you? How could he make you laugh, poor child?"

Constance.—"Oh, it's a long story. It was all through my bewilderment at his resemblance. It confused me. I kept thinking it was he,—as if it were some dream,—and whenever this one mentioned some trait of his that totally differed from his, don't you know, I got more and more confused, and—mamma!"—with sudden desolation—"I know he knows all about it!"

Mrs. Wyatt.—"I am sure he doesn't. Mr. Cummings only told him that his resemblance was a painful association. He assured your father of this, and wouldn't hear a word more. I'm certain you're wrong. But what made you think he knows?"

Constance solemnly.—"He behaved just as if he didn't."

Mrs. Wyatt.—"Ah, you can't judge from that, my dear." Impressively: "Men are very different."

Constance, doubtfully.—"Do you think so, mamma?"

Mrs. Wyatt.—"I'm certain of it."

Constance, after a pause.—"Mamma, will you help take this shawl off my feet? I am so warm. I think I should like to walk about a little. Can you see the island from the gallery?"

Mrs. Wyatt.—"Do you think you'd better try to leave your chair, Constance?"

Constance.—"Yes, I'm stronger this morning. And I shall never gain, lounging about this way." She begins to loose the wraps from her feet, and Mrs. Wyatt coming doubtfully to her aid she is presently freed. She walks briskly towards the sofa, and sits down quite erectly in the corner of it. "There! that's pleasanter. I get so tired of being a burden." She is silent, and then she begins softly and wearily to laugh again.

Mrs. Wyatt, smiling curiously.—"What is it, Constance? I don't at all understand what made you laugh."

Constance.—"Why, don't you know? Several times after I had been surprised that he didn't like this thing, and hadn't that habit and the other, he noticed it, and pretended that it was an attempt at mind-reading, and then all at once he turned and said I must try once more, and he asked, 'Do I like smoking?' and I said instantly, 'Oh, yes!' Why, it was like having a whole tobacconist's shop in the same room with you from the moment he came in; and of course he understood what I meant, and blushed, and then felt for his handkerchief, and pulled it out, and discharged a perfect volley of pipes and tobacco, that seemed to be tangled up in it, all over the floor, and then I began to laugh—so silly, so disgusting; so perfectly flat! and I thought I should die, it was so ridiculous! and—Oh, dear, I'm beginning again!" She hides her face in her handkerchief and leans her head on the back of the sofa : "Say something, do something to stop me, mother!" She stretches an imploring left hand toward the elder lady, who still remains apparently but half convinced of any reason for mirth, when General Wyatt, hastily entering, pauses in abrupt irresolution at the spectacle of Constance's passion.

IV.
GENERAL WYATT, CONSTANCE, and MRS. WYATT.

Constance.—"Oh, ha, ha, ha! Oh, ha, ha, ha, ha!"

General Wyatt—"Margaret! Constance!" At the sound of his voice, Constance starts up with a little cry, and stiffens into an attitude of ungracious silence, without looking at her father, who turns with an expression of pain toward her mother.

Mrs. Wyatt.—"Yes, James. We were laughing at something Constance had been telling me about Mr. Bartlett. Tell your father, Constance."

Constance, coldly, while she draws through her hand the handkerchief which she has been pressing to her eyes.—"I don't think it would amuse papa." She passes her hand across her lap, and does not lift her heavy eye-lashes.

Mrs. Wyatt, caressingly.—"Oh, yes, it would; I'm sure it would."

Constance.—"You can tell it then, mamma."

Mrs. Wyatt.—"No; you, my dear. You tell it so funnily; and "—in a lower tone—" it's so long since your father heard you laugh."

Constance.—"There was nothing funny in it. It was disgusting. I was laughing from nervousness."

Mrs. Wyatt.—"Why, Constance"—

General Wyatt.—"Never mind, Margaret. Another time will do." He chooses to ignore the coldness of his daughter's bearing toward himself. "I came to see if Constance were not strong enough to go out on the lake this morning. The boats are very good, and the air is so fine that I think she'll be the better for it. Mr. Bartlett is going out to the island to sketch, and "—

Constance.—"I don't care to go."

Mrs. Wyatt.—"Do go, my daughter! I know it will do you good."

Constance.—"I am not strong enough."

Mrs. Wyatt.—"But you said you were better, just now; and you should yield to to your father's judgment."

Constance.—"I will do whatever papa bids me."

General Wyatt—"I don't bid you. Margaret, I think I will go out with Mr. Bartlett. We will be back at dinner." He turns and leaves the room without looking again at Constance.

V.
CONSTANCE and MRS. WYATT; then BARTLETT.

Mrs. Wyatt.—"Oh, Constance! How can you treat your father so coldly? You will suffer some day for the pain you give him!"

Constance.—"Suffer? No, I'm past that. I've exhausted my power of suffering."

Mrs. Wyatt.—"You haven't exhausted your power of making others suffer."

Constance, crouching listlessly down upon the sofa.—"I told you that I lived only to give pain. But it's my fate, not my will. Nothing but that can excuse me."

Mrs. Wyatt, wringing her hands.—"Oh, oh! Well, then, give me pain if you must torment somebody. But spare your father,—spare the heart that loves you so tenderly, you unhappy girl."

Constance, with hardness.—"Whenever I see papa, my first thought is, If he had not been so harsh and severe, it might never have happened! What can I care for his loving me when he hated him? Oh, I will do my duty, mother; I will obey; I have obeyed, and I know how. Papa can't demand anything of me now that isn't easy. I have forgiven everything, and if you give me time I can forget. I have forgotten. I have been laughing at something so foolish, it ought to make me cry for shame."

Mrs. Wyatt.—"Constance, you try me beyond all endurance! You talk of forgiving, you talk of forgetting, you talk of that wretch! Forgive him, forget him, if you can. If he had been half a man, if he had ever cared a tithe as much for you as for himself, all the hate of all the fathers in the world could not have driven him from you. You talk of obeying"—

Mary, the serving woman, flying into the room.—"Oh, please, Mrs. Wyatt! There are four men carrying somebody up the hill. And General Wyatt just went down, and I can't see him anywhere, and"—

Mrs. Wyatt—"You're crazy, Mary! He hasn't been gone a moment; there isn't time; it can't be he!" Mrs. Wyatt rushes to the gallery that overlooks the road to verify her hope or fear, and then out of one of the doors into the corridor, while Constance springs frantically to her feet and runs toward the other door.

Constance.—"Oh, yes, yes! It's papa! It's my dear, good, kind papa! He's dead; he's drowned; I drove him away; I murdered him! Ah-h-h-h!" She shrinks back with a shriek at sight of Bartlett, whose excited face appears at the door.—"Go! It was you, you who made me hate my father! You made me kill him, and now I abhor you! I"—

Bartlett—"Wait! Hold on! What is it all?"

Constance.—"Oh, forgive me! I didn't mean—I didn't know it was you, sir! But where is he? Oh, take me to him! Is he dead?" She seizes his arm, and clings to it trembling.

Bartlett—"Dead? No, he isn't dead. He was knocked over by a team coming behind him down the hill, and was slightly bruised. There's no cause for alarm. He sent me to tell you; they've carried him to your rooms."

Constance.—"Oh, thank Heaven!" She a bows her head with a sob, upon his shoulder, and then lifts her tearful eyes to his; "Help me to get to him! I am weak." She totters and Bartlett mechanically passes a supporting arm about her. "Help me, and don't—don't leave me!" She moves with him a few paces toward the door, her head drooping; but all at once she raises her face again, stares at him, stiffly releases herself, and with a long look of reproach walks proudly away to the other door, by which she vanishes without a word.

Bartlett, remaining planted, with a bewildered glance at his empty arm: "Well, I wonder who and what and where I am!"

III.
DISSOLVING VIEWS.

I.
GENERAL WYATT and MRS. WYATT.

In the parlour stands an easel with a canvas of inordinate dimensions upon it, and near this a small table, with a fresh box of colours in tubes, and a holiday outfit of new brushes, pallet, and other artist's materials, evidently not the property of Bartlett. Across the room from this apparatus is stretched Constance's easy-chair, towards which General Wyatt, bearing some marks of his recent accident in a bandaged wrist and a stiff leg, stumps heavily, supported by Mrs. Wyatt. Beside this chair is the centre-table of the parlour, on which are an open box of cigars, and a pile of unopened newspapers.

General Wyatt, dropping into the chair with a groan.—"Well, my dear! I feel uncommonly ashamed of myself, taking Constance's chair in this manner. Though there's a great consolation in thinking she doesn't need it any longer." Settling himself more comfortably in the chair, and laying his stick across his knees : "Margaret, I begin to be very happy about Constance. I haven't had so light a heart for many a long day. The last month has made a wonderful change in her. She is almost like her old self again."

Mrs. Wyatt, sighing.—"Yes, it seems almost too good to be true. I don't know quite what to make of it. Sometimes, I almost fear for her mind. I'm sure that half the time she forgets that Mr. Bartlett isn't that wretch, and I can see her awake with a start to the reality every little while, and then wilfully lull her consciousness to sleep again. He's terribly like, I can hardly keep from crying out at times; and yesterday I did give way: I was so ashamed, and he looked so hurt. I see Constance restrain herself often, and I dare say there are times that we don't know of when she doesn't."

General Wyatt.—"Well, all that may be. But it's a thing that will right itself in time. We must do our best not to worry him. This painter is a fine fellow, my dear. I took a great fancy to him at the beginning. I liked him from the moment I saw him."

Mrs. Wyatt.—"James! You were going to strike him with your cane."

General Wyatt.—"That was before I saw him. I was going to strike the other one. But that's neither here nor there. We must be careful not to hurt his feelings; that's all. We've got our Constance back again, Margaret. Impossible as it seems, we have got her back by his help. Isn't it wonderful to see that killing weight lifted from her young life? It's like a miracle."

Mrs. Wyatt.—"It isn't lifted all the time, James."

General Wyatt.—"No matter—no matter. It isn't crushing her all the time either. I'm glad for what relief there is, and I feel that all is going well. Do you hear that step, Margaret? Listen! That's like the old bounding tread of our little girl. Where is the leaden-footed phantom that used to drag along that hall? Is she coming this way?"

Mrs. Wyatt, listening.—"No, she is going to our rooms. Has Mr. Bartlett been here yet?"

General Wyatt.—"Not yet. He was to come when he got back from his sketching. What a good fellow, to take so much trouble for Constance's amusement! It was uncommonly kind of Mr. Bartlett, Margaret, offering to give her these lessons."

Mrs. Wyatt.—"Yes, it worries me."

General Wyatt.—"Why in the world should it worry you, Margaret?"

Mrs. Wyatt.—"You can't offer him any compensation for his instructions."

General Wyatt—"Of course not. That would be offensive. Well?"

Mrs. Wyatt.—"Well, James, can't you see how it complicates everything? He is conferring another obligation. He might almost think we tried to throw them together."

General Wyatt, fiercely.—"He had better not! Why, Margaret, he's a gentleman! He can't think that."

Mrs. Wyatt.—"No, I suppose not. I suppose it's our trouble that has made me suspicious of every one." She goes sadly about the room, rearranging, with a house-keeper's instinct, everything in it.

General Wyatt.—"You needn't trouble yourself with the room, Margaret; Mary told me that she and the landlady had put it in order."

Mrs. Wyatt.—"That's just why I need." After a moment: "Are you going to be here, James?"

General Wyatt.—"Yes, I thought I should stay. It's a cheerful place to read and smoke. It won't disturb them, will it?"

Mrs. Wyatt.—"Oh, no! It's quite necessary some one should stay. I'm very glad you can, for I've got a few little things to do."

General Wyatt.—"All right. I'll stay and do the dragon, or whatever it is. But I wish you hadn't put it in that light, Margaret. I was proposing to enjoy myself."

Mrs. Wyatt.—"Enjoy yourself, James? With such a terribly perplexing affair before you!"

General Wyatt.—"I don't see anything perplexing about it. It's perfectly simple, to my mind. Mr. Bartlett kindly proposes to give Constance a few lessons in drawing,—or painting; I don't know which it is. That's the beginning and the end of it."

Mrs. Wyatt, with a heavy sigh.—"Yes, that's the beginning."

General Wyatt, impatiently.—"Well?"

Mrs. Wyatt—"Nothing. Are you quite comfortable, here? Have you got every-thing you wish?"

General Wyatt, with a glance at the things on the table at his elbow.—"Here are my cigars, and—yes, here are the papers. Yes, I'm all right. But what do you mean by 'nothing'? What—Ah, here's Mr.Bartlett!" As Bartlett comes into the room, the General, since he cannot conveniently rise, makes a demonstration of welcome with his hands. Bartlett has his colour-box under his arm, and a canvas in his hand. "You've been improving the shining hour, I see, What have you there?"

II.
BARTLETT, GENERAL WYATT, and MRS, WYATT.

Bartlett, with a smile and nod inclusive of Mrs. Wyatt.—"Nothing worth looking at." He goes and faces it against the wall. "Have I kept Miss Wyatt waiting?"

Mrs. Wyatt, anxiously.—"It's too bad you should waste your time upon her, Mr. Bartlett. I don't know why we let you."

Bartlett—"You can't help yourself, Mrs. Wyatt. The wrong is owing to circumstances beyond your control. If I have any virtue it is a particularly offensive form of stubbornness. Besides,"—more seriously,—"I feel myself honoured to do it—to contribute anything to Miss Wyatt's—ah—ah—In short, if she can stand it I can."

General Wyatt.—"It's immensely kind of you. By the way, you won't mind my staying here, will you, to read my papers, while you're at work? Because if you do, I can clear out at once." Mrs. Wyatt, with mute but lively tokens of dismay, attends the General's further remarks: "I don't want to stay here and be a bore and a nuisance, you know." Mrs. Wyatt vanishes from the scene in final despair.

Bartlett, going up to the easel and dragging it into an entirely new position.— "Not in the least. Some woman been putting this room in order, hasn't there?"

General Wyatt.—"Three."

Bartlett—"I thought so." He continues to disarrange all the preparations for his work. His operations bring him in the vicinity of General Wyatt, upon whose box of cigars his eye falls, "Oh, I say, General! Smoking?"

General Wyatt.—"Certainly. Why not?"

Bartlett—"Well, I don't know. I thought perhaps—I supposed—I imagined somehow from something she said, or that happened—it was offensive to Miss Wyatt."

General Wyatt—"Why, bless your heart, man, she minds it no more than I do!"

Bartlett—"You don't say so! Why, I haven't smoked any for the last two weeks, because—because—And I'm almost dead for a pipe!"

General Wyatt—"Why, poor fellow! Why, here! Take a cigar!"

Bartlett, significantly shaking his head.—"Oh, no, no! I said a pipe." He rushes to an old studio jacket which the landlady has hung for him on the back of a chair; he dives in one pocket and gets out a pipe, plunges into another and extracts a pouch of tobacco. He softly groans and murmurs with impatience while he makes these explorations. Upon their success : "So lucky Mrs. Ransom brought down that coat. I couldn't have lived to get up-stairs after it!" Stuffing his pipe in a frenzy, he runs to the General for a match; that veteran has already lighted it, and extends it toward him. Bartlett stoops over the flame, pipe in mouth. As the General drops the extinct match upon the floor the painter puffs a great cloud, in which involved he is putting on his studio jacket when Constance appears at the door. He instinctively snatches his pipe from his lips and puts it in his pocket.

III.
CONSTANCE, BARTLETT, and GENERAL WYATT.

Constance, fighting her way through the smoke to the General's chair.—"Why, papa, how you have been smoking!"

General Wyatt, with a queer look,—"Yes, I find it rests me after a bad night, I didn't sleep well."

Constance.—"Oh, poor papa! How do you do, Mr. Bartlett?" She gives him her hand for good-morning.

Bartlett.—"Oh, quite well, quite well now, thank you. I—I—had been a little off my—diet."

Constance.—"Oh!"

Bartlett—"Yes. But I've gone back now, and I'm all right again." He retires to the easel, and mechanically resumes his pipe, but takes it from his mouth again, and after an impatient glance at it, throws it out of the window. "When you're ready, Miss Wyatt, we can begin any time. There's no hurry, though."

Constance.—"I'm ready now. Is everything in reach, papa?"

General Wyatt.—"Yes, my dear. I'm so perfectly comfortable that one touch more would make me miserable."

Constance.—"Can't I do something for you?"

General Wyatt.—"Not a thing. I'm a prodigy of content."

Constance.—"Not lift up this last fold of the chair, so your foot won't rest so heavily on the floor?"

General Wyatt.—"Was it resting heavily? I hadn't noticed. Yes, it was; how you see everything, my dear! Yes"—Constance stoops to put up the chair to its last extension, and Bartlett runs forward to anticipate her.

Bartlett.—"Miss Wyatt, let me do that!"

Constance.—"No, no! No one must touch papa but me. There, is that right, papa?"

General Wyatt.—"Exactly. That makes me pluperfectly comfortable. I haven't a wish in the world, and all I ask now is to"—

Constance.—"Get at your newspapers? Let me take off the wrappers for you."

General Wyatt.—"Not on any account." He gently withdraws from her the newspaper she has taken up. "That is truly a kindness that kills. Open my papers for me? I'd as lief you'd put on my hat for me, my dear."

Bartlett.—"That's the one thing that can't be done for any man!"

Constance.—"Why not? A woman can put on another woman's bonnet for her."

General Wyatt.—"Ah, that's a different thing. A man doesn't wear his hat for looks."

Constance.—"That's true, papa,—some of them." She turns gaily from her father, and looks up at Bartlett, who has smilingly listened. She gives a start, and suppresses a cry; she passes her hand quickly over her eyes, and then staying herself a moment with one hand on the back of a chair resumes with forced calm : "Shall we begin, now—ah—Mr.—Bartlett?" An awkward silence ensues, in which Bartlett remains frowning, and the General impatiently flings open a newspaper. Then Bartlett's frown relaxes into a compassionate response to her appealing look.

Bartlett.—"Yes, I'm quite ready. But it's you who are to begin, Miss Wyatt. I am to assume the safe and eligible position of art critic. I wish I had some of those fellows who write about my pictures before an easel; I'd stand their unpleasant company a while for the sake of taking the conceit out of them. Not but what my pictures are bad enough,—as bad as any critic says, for that matter. Well, Miss Wyatt; here is the charcoal, and yonder out-doors is the mountain."

Constance.—"Excuse me a moment. Papa, will our talking disturb you?" To Bartlett : "I suppose we will have to talk a little?"

Bartlett.—"A little."

General Wyatt, from behind his paper.—"It won't disturb me if you don't talk to me."

Constance.—"We'll try not." To Bartlett : "Well?"

Bartlett, as Constance places herself before the canvas, and receiving the charcoal from his fingers, glances out at Ponkwasset.—

"May I ask why you chose such a capacious canvas?"

Constance, in meek surprise.—"Why, the mountain being a large object"—

Bartlett.—"A large canvas was necessary. I see. There's reason in that. But were you going to do it life size?"

Constance, as before.—"Why, no!"

Bartlett.—"What was your idea?"

Constance.—"I don't know. I thought—I thought I would have the mountain in the back-ground, with some clouds over it, and a few figures in the foreground, to give it a human interest."

Bartlett.—"Yes, that's a good notion, Well, now begin. First get your distance— No; better strike in a horizon line first. That will keep you right. Draw the line straight across the middle of the canvas." Constance retires a few steps from the canvas, measures its spaces with her eye, and then with a glance at the horizon outside draws. Bartlett, looking over her shoulder: "Straight, straight! The line should be straight. Don't you see?"

Constance, falteringly.—"I meant that for a straight line."

Bartlett—"Oh! well! Yes! I see. However, now you've got it in, hadn't you better use it for a curved line? Say for that wavering outline of the hills beyond Ponkwasset?"

Constance.—"Why, if you think so, Mr, Bartlett."

Bartlett.—"And I'll just strike in the horizon line here." He draws rapidly, steps back a pace, approaches, and touches Constance's line at different points. Then he gives her the chalk again. "Now, scratch in the outline of Ponkwasset." Constance begins to draw. "Ah! Wait a moment, please. You're not quite getting it. Will you let me?" Constance offers him the charcoal, which he declines with a gesture, "No, no! You must do it. I meant"—

Constance.—"What?"

Bartlett—"That if you would allow me to—to—guide your hand"—

Constance, frankly.—"Why, of course. Do what you like with it"—

Bartlett.—"Oh!"

Constance.—"So that you teach it a little of the skill of yours." He gently, and after some delicate hesitations, takes her hand, as it grasps the charcoal, and slowly guides it in forming the outline of the mountain. Constance, in admiration of his cleverness : "What a delicious touch you have!"

Bartlett, confusedly.—"Yes?"

Constance, regarding the outline after he has released her hand, while Bartlett, with a gesture of rapturous fondness, looks at the fingers that have guided hers, and tenderly kisses them.—"Oh, yes : I'd give anything if I had your hand!"

Bartlett.—"It's at your service always, Miss Wyatt."

Constance, still regarding the picture.—"Ah, but I should need your mind, too!"

Bartlett—"Well?"

Constance.—"I couldn't rob you of everything." She begins to draw again, and then, in pretty, unconscious imitation of Bartlett, throws back her head.

Bartlett, breaking forth in rapture at her movement and attitude.—"Oh, divine!"

Constance, innocently beaming upon him.—"Do you think so? I didn't suppose I could get it so at once. Is it really good?"

Bartlett, recalled to himself.—"Who? What? Yes, yes; it isn't bad. Not at all bad. That is"—

Constance, disappointedly.—"I thought you liked it." Gravely : "Why did you say it was divine?"

Bartlett—"Because—I—I—thought so!"

Constance, with mystification.—"I'm afraid I don't understand. Shall I let this outline remain for Ponkwasset, or shall I use it for something else?"

Bartlett.—"Yes, let it remain for Ponkwasset; if it needs changing that can easily be done afterwards. Now block out your middle distance. So!" He takes the charcoal from her and draws. "Now, then, sketch in your figures."

Constance, timidly.—"How large shall I make them?"

Bartlett.—"Oh, as large as you like. How large did you think?"

Constance.—"I don't know. About a foot high."

Bartlett—"Well, try them." Constance draws, and Bartlett regards the operation with gestures and contortions of countenance expressive of mingled tenderness for Constance and extreme suffering from her performance. She turns about, and surprises him with his hands clutched in his shaggy hair.

Constance, with dignity.—"What is the matter, Mr. Bartlett?"

Bartlett, forcing an imbecile smile.—"Nothing, I was just thinking—I should—like to venture to make a remark."

Constance.—"You know I wish you to speak to me about everything."

Bartlett.—"Did you mean that lady to be in the middle distance?"

Constance.—"Yes."

Bartlett—"Well, there is a slight, a very slight, error in the perspective. She is as tall as Ponkwasset, you see, and could touch the top of it with the point of her parasol."

Constance, dejectedly.—"I see, I can never do it."

Bartlett.—"Oh, yes, you can, Miss Wyatt; you mustn't lose patience with me."

Constance.—"It's you who won't be able to keep your patience with my stupidity."

Bartlett.—"That's not the name for it. I shall think more of your failures than of anybody's successes—that is—I mean—if you don't let this thing be a pain instead of a pleasure to you. Remember, I hoped it would amuse you."

Constance,—"Oh, yes. You have been only too kind, in that and everything."

Bartlett.—"Well, now, let us begin again. This lady is very well as a lady; you understand the figure better than perspective; but she's out of place here, a little; and a flower out of place, you know, is a weed. Suppose we"—he takes up the charcoal, and makes a few dashes at the canvas—"treat her as a clump of tall birch-trees,—that clump over there in the edge of the meadow; that will bring her into the foreground, and entitle her to be three inches high; we can't really allow her more, even as a clump of birches. Eh?"

Constance.—"Oh, yes; that's better, decidedly." Smiling: "Being under instruction, this way, makes me think of my school-days."

Bartlett, impressively.—"I hope they were happy days."

Constance.—"Oh, the happiest of my life."

Bartlett—"I am so glad." Constance stares at him in surprise, but finally says nothing. "I mean since this is like them."

Constance, pensively.—"Yes, it's pleasant to go back to that time." With more animation : "Papa, I wonder if you remember Madame Le May, who used to teach me French when you came home after the war?"

General Wyatt, behind his newspaper.—"Eh? What? What's that? Some difficulty in the drawing? You must both have patience,—patience"—

Constance.—"Why, papa! Oh, well, I won't worry him. I suppose he's found something about cutting down the army appropriations; that always absorbs him. What shall I try next, Mr. Bartlett?"

Bartlett.—"You can rub in your middle distance."

Constance, laughing.—"I'll try. But I think I should be at my best beyond the vanishing point."

Bartlett.—"Oh, I don't believe that! Perhaps it annoys you to have me looking over your shoulder while you work?"

Constance.—"No. Oh, no."

Bartlett—"I see that it does."

Constance.—"It makes me a little nervous. I m afraid of you, you know."

Bartlett.—"I didn't know I was so terrible. How far off shall I go, to be agreeable?"

Constance, laughing.—"Across the room."

Bartlett.—"Shall you like me better at that distance?"

Constance.—"I can't let you make a joke of our liking for you."

Bartlett.—"You defend me, even in my presence. What kindhess I must miss when I'm absent! Well, I will go and see what interests General Wyatt."

General Wyatt.—"Madame Le May? Yes, certainly. Remember her perfectly. False hair, false teeth, false"—

Constance.—"Why, what are you talking of, papa?"

General Wyatt.—"Mayo. Capital cavalry officer—cutting down the pay of such a man"—

Constance.—"What are you reading?" The General makes no answer.

Bartlett.—"Don't disturb him. I'll walk off here at this end of the room." He paces softly up and down, while Constance returns to her drawing, to which she diligently applies herself. A thought seems to strike Bartlett as his wandering eye falls upon General Wyatt, who still sits with his head buried in his newspaper. He approaches, and remarks in a low tone : "I believe I will take a cigar now, Gen—" The newspaper falls slightly, and Bartlett makes a discovery. The General has dropped off into a doze. With a gesture of amusement, Bartlett restores the paper to its place, and resumes his walk in a quiet rapture, interrupting it now and then to dwell in silent adoration on the young lady's absorption in the fine arts.

Constance.—"Mr. Bartlett"—

Bartlett, halting.—"Recalled from exile already? Well?"

Constance.—"I'm afraid I can't get by this point alone."

Bartlett—"Yes? Let's see it." He eagerly crosses the room, takes his stand behind her, and throws up his hands in despair. Constance indicates her difficulties,

Constance.—"The question is how to get in some idea of those slopes of the mountain. These things seem to crowd everything out."

Bartlett, hopelessly regarding the work.—"I see. You have been composing a little,—idealising. Well, I don't object to that. Though perhaps it had better come later. This long stretch of rocky cliff"—

Constance.—"Rocky cliff?"

Bartlett.—"Isn't in nature, but it might have a good effect if properly utilised"—

Constance.—"But it isn't rocky cliff, Mr. Bartlett. It's"—

Bartlett, looking a second time, and more closely.—"Why, of course! It's that stretch of broken woodland at the foot of the mountain. Very good; very good indeed; very boldly treated. Still, I should say"—

Constance, in desperation.—"Oh, Mr. Bartlett, it isn't rocks, and it isn't woods; it's—hay-stacks!"

Bartlett.—"Hay-stacks?"

Constance, desolately.—"Yes, hay-stacks."

Bartlett.—"But hay-stacks at the foot of the mountain, Miss Wyatt"—

Constance, inconsolably.—"They're not at the foot of the mountain. They're those hay-stacks just out there in the meadow. I thought it would be nice to have them in near that clump of birches you drew."

Bartlett.—"Oh-h-h-h!" He scratches his head in visible stupefaction. Then with re-animation : "I see. It was my error. I was looking for middle distance, and you had been working on the foreground. Very good; very—Oh, gracious powers—No, no! Don't be discouraged, Miss Wyatt; remember it's the first time you've attempted anything of the sort, and you've really done very well. Here!" He seizes the pencil and draws, "We will just sink these hay-stacks,—which are very good in their way, but not perhaps sufficiently subordinated,—just sink them into the lake yonder. They will serve very well for the reflections of those hills beyond, and now you can work away at some of the details of the foreground; they will interest you more." He retires a pace, "It's really not a bad start as it is."

Constance, ruefully.—"But it's all yours, Mr. Bartlett."

Bartlett—"Eh?"

Constance.—"You drew every line in it."

Bartlett.—"No, you drew the line of the distant hills."

Constance.—"But I didn't mean it for that!"

Bartlett—"Well, well; but the lady's figure, that was good"—

Constance.—"You turned her into a clump of birches."

Bartlett.—"True. A mere exigency of the perspective. The hay-stacks"—

Constance.—"You've just sunk them into the lake!"

Bartlett.—"Well, well. Perhaps I may have helped in the execution of the picture, a little. But my dear Miss Wyatt, the drawing is nothing; it's the design is what makes the picture, and that's entirely yours; the ideas were all yours. Come! Try your hand now at the shore line of the lake, just here."

Constance.—"I'm afraid I'm a little tired. My hands are cold."

Bartlett—"Oh, I'm sorry!" He takes one of them and places it between either of his. " That shows you've been working too hard. I can't allow that. All the art in the world isn't worth—I mustn't forget that you have not been well; and I want these little lessons to be a pastime and not a burden to you. The picture's sufficiently advanced now"—he mechanically puts her hand under his left arm, and keeps his own right hand upon it, while he takes his station with her in front of the easel—"to warrant us in trying a little colour to-morrow. You'll be very much more interested in colour. It is refreshing to get at the brushes after you've tired yourself out with the black and white. You've got a very pretty outfit, there, Miss Wyatt." He indicates her colours on the little table.

Constance.—"I didn't mean to refuse the offer of your paints, but I thought it would be better to have the colours perfectly fresh, you know."

Bartlett.—"Quite right. Quite right. Now you see—Rest on me, Miss Wyatt, or I shall be afraid of fatiguing you by standing; and I'd like to point out a few things for you to begin on here to-morrow."

Constance.—"Oh, I'm not very tired. But I will keep your arm if you will let me."

Bartlett, making her sustain her weight more distinctly on his arm.—"By all means. Now, here, at this point, I think I'd better sketch you in that old oak down there at the foot of our hill, with its grape-vine, and you can work away at these without reference to Ponkwasset. The line of that clinging vine is one of the most graceful things that Nature—and Nature does know a thing or two, Miss Wyatt; she's particularly good at clinging vines—ever drew." He looks at her over his shoulder with an involuntary sigh. Then, "Suppose"—he takes up the charcoal—"I do it now. No, don't disturb yourself." They lean forward, and as he sketches, their faces, drawn together, almost touch. Bartlett drops the pencil, and starts away, releasing his arm : "Oh, no, no!"

Constance, simply.—"Can't you do it?"

Bartlett, in deep emotion.—"No, no; I can't do it—I mustn't—it would be outrageous—I—I"—Regaining his self-possession at sight of Constance's astonished face : "You said yourself just now that I had drawn everything in the picture. I can't do any more. You must do the clinging vine!"

Constance, innocently.—"Very well, I'll try. If you'll do the oak for me. I'll let you do that much more." They regard each other, she with her innocent smile, he with a wild rapture of hope, doubt, and fear. Then Bartlett draws a long, despairing sigh, and turns away.

Bartlett—"To-morrow, to-morrow!" He walks away, and returns to her, "Have you read—have you ever read The Talking Oak, Miss Wyatt?"

Constance.—"Tennyson's? A thousand times. Isn't it charming?"

Bartlett.—"It's absurd, I think. Do you remember where he makes the oak say of the young lady,—

'And in a fit of frolic mirth She strove to span my waist: . . . . I wish'd myself the fair young beech That here beside me stands, That round me, clasping each in each, She might have lock'd her hands'?"

Constance.—"Why, that's lovely,—that attribution of human feeling to the tree. Don't you think so?"

Bartlett, absently.—"Yes, yes; beautiful. But it's terrible, too; terrible. Supposing the oak really had human feeling; or supposing that a man had been meant in the figure of an oak"—He has drawn near Constance again; but now he retreats. "Ah, I can't work out the idea."

Constance.—"What idea? I can't imagine what you mean."

Bartlett.—"Ah! I can. My trouble is, I can't say what I mean! This was some time a paradox."

Constance.—"Oh! I should think, a riddle."

Bartlett.—"Some day I hope you'll let me read it to you."

Constance.—"Why not now?"

Bartlett, impetuously.—"If you only meant what you said, it would be—so much better than if I said what I meant!"

Constance.—"You are dealing in mysteries to-day."

Bartlett—"Oh, the greatest of them! But don't mind. Wait! I'll try to tell you what I mean. I won't make you stand, while I talk. Here!" He wheels up in front of the picture one of the haircloth sofas; Constance mechanically sinks down upon it, and he takes his place at her side; she bends upon him a look of smiling amusement. "I can put my meaning best, I think, in the form of allegory. Do you like allegory, Miss Wyatt?"

Constance.—"Yes. That is, not very much."

Bartlett—"Oh! You don't like allegory! Upon second thoughts, I don't myself. We will not try allegory. We will try a supposed case. I think that's always the best way, don't you?"

Constance.—"No, I don't like any sort of indirection. I believe the straightforward way is the best."

Bartlett.—"Yes, so do I; but it's impossible. We must try a supposed case."

Constance, laughing.—"Well!"

Bartlett—"Ah! I can't say anything if you laugh. It's a serious matter."

Constance, with another burst of laughter.—"I should never have thought so." With a sudden return of her old morbid mood: "I beg your pardon for laughing. What right have I to laugh? Go on, Mr. Bartlett, and I will listen as I should have done. I am ashamed."

Bartlett.—"No, no! That won't do! You mustn't take me so seriously as that! Oh, Miss Wyatt, if I could only be so much your friend, your fool,—I don't care what,—as to banish that look, that tone from you for ever!"

Constance.—"Why do you care?"

Bartlett.—"Why do I care? "

Constance.—"Yes. Why should you mind whether so weak and silly a thing as I is glad or sad? I can't understand. Why have you had so much patience with me? Why do you take all this trouble on my account, and waste your time on me? Why"—

Bartlett, starting up.—"Why do I do it?" He walks away to the other side of the room with signs of great inward struggle; then he swiftly returns to her side where she has risen and stands near the sofa, and seizes her hand. "Well, I will tell you why. No, no! I can't! It would be"—

General Wyatt, behind his newspaper.—"Outrageous! Gross violation of good faith! Infernal shame!" The General concludes these observations with a loud, pro-longed, and very stertorous respiration.

Constance, running to him.—"Why, papa, what do you mean? Oh poor papa! He's asleep, and in such a wretched position!" From which she hastens to move him, while Bartlett, recovering from the amaze in which the appositeness of the General's remarks had plunged him, breaks into a harsh "Ha! ha!" Constance turns and advances upon him in threatening majesty : "Did you laugh, Mr. Bartlett?"

Bartlett, after a moment's dismay.—"Well, I don't know whether you call it laughing. I smiled."

Constance, with increasing awfulness: "Why did you laugh, Mr. Bartlett?"

Bartlett.—"I—I—I can't say."

Constance.—"You were laughing at General Wyatt!"

Bartlett.—"Was there nothing to laugh at?"

Constance.—"For children! For vulgar, silly boys! For a gentleman, nothing!"

Bartlett, with rising wrath.—"Then I have no excuse, unless I say that I am no gentleman."

Constance.—"I shall not dispute you in anything; and I will leave you to the enjoyment of your mirth."

Bartlett.—"Very well. As you like. I am sorry to have offended you. I shall take care never to offend you again." Constance sweeps towards one door, at the thresh-old of which she pauses to look round and see Bartlett dashing her box of colours together as if it were his own, and thrusting it under his arm, seizing with a furious hand the canvas on the easel and his coat from the chair-back, and then rushing from the room. She drops her face into her hands and vanishes, and the next moment Mrs. Wyatt enters.

IV.
MRS. WYATT and GENERAL WYATT.

Mrs. Wyatt.—"What is the matter with Constance, James? Have you been"—She goes up to the General and discovers his vigilance: "Asleep!" Waking him : "James, James! Is this the way you do the dragon, as you call it?"

General Wyatt, starting awake : "Dragon? Dragon? What dragon? I dreamt I was a perfect fiery dragon, and went about breathing flame and smoke. How long have I slept, Margaret? Where is Mr. Bartlett? Where is Constance?"

Mrs. Wyatt.—"Oh, you may well ask that, James. I just met Constance at the door, in tears. Oh, I hope nothing dreadful has happened."

General Wyatt.—"Nonsense, Margaret. Here, help me up, my dear. My nap hasn't done me any good. I'm stiff all over."

Mrs. Wyatt, anxiously.—"I'm afraid you have taken cold, James."

General Wyatt, with impatience.—"Cold? No! Not in the least. I'm perfectly well. But that was a very unpleasant dream. Margaret, I'm afraid that I breathed rather—explosively, at one time."

Mrs. Wyatt—"Oh, James, this is worse and worse. It must have mortified Constance, dreadfully."

General Wyatt, taking his wife's arm, and limping from the scene :—"Well, well! Never mind! I'll make it right with Bartlett. He's a man of sense, and will help me laugh it off with her. It will be all right, Margaret; don't worry over a trifle like that."

Mrs. Wyatt, as they disappear :—"Trifle? Her whole happiness may depend upon it." At the instant of their withdrawal, Constance and Bartlett, hastily entering by opposite doors, encounter each other in the middle of the room.

V.
BARTLETT and CONSTANCE

Both, at once.—"I came to"—

Bartlett.—"Restore you your box of colours and your canvas, which I carried off by mistake,"

Constance.—"To say that I am very, very sorry for my rudeness to you, and to entreat you to forget my abominable words, if you can."

Bartlett, with a generous rush of emotion, dropping the canvas on the floor at one side and the box of colours on the other, and snatching her extended hand to his lips.—"Don't say that. I deserved a thousand times more. You were right."

Constance.—"No, no! I can't let you blame yourself to save me from self-reproach. I know papa was ridiculous. But what made me angry was this thought that you were laughing at him. I couldn't bear that. I shouldn't have minded your laughing at me; but at papa!"

Bartlett, sadly.—"I happened to be laughing much more at myself than your father. Where is the General?"

Constance.—"He has gone with mamma. They wondered where you were, and I said you were coming back again."

Bartlett.—"How did you know?"

Constance.—"I thought you would come,—that you would upbraid yourself for my bad behaviour, and return to excuse it to me. You see what perfect faith I—we—have in you."

Bartlett, earnestly.—"Have you indeed perfect faith in me?"

Constance.—"Perfect!"

Bartlett, vehemently.—"But why, why do you trust me? You see that I am hasty and rude."

Constance.—"Oh no, not rude."

Bartlett.—"But I assure you that I am so; and you have seen that I laughed—that I am wanting in delicacy, and"—

Constance, devoutly.—"How can you say that to us, when every day, every hour, every instant of the last month has given us proof of unimaginable kindness in you!" He eagerly approaches and takes her hands, which she frankly yields him. "Your patience, your noble forbearance, which we so sorely tried, has made us all forget that you are a stranger, and—and—to me it's as if we had always known you"—her head droops—"as if you were a—an old friend, a brother"—

Bartlett, dropping her hands.—"Oh!" He turns away, and pacing the length of the room reapproaches her hastily.

Constance, with a little cry.—"Mr. Bartlett! Do look! Did you intend to trample my canvas and colours under foot?" She makes as if to stoop for them.

Bartlett, his manner undergoing a total change as if he had been suddenly recalled to himself at a critical moment.—"Don't!" He hastily picks them up, and puts the canvas on the easel and the colours on the table. With a glance at the canvas: "Ponkwasset doesn't seem to have been seriously injured by his violent usage. Shall you like to try your hand at him again tomorrow?"

Constance.—"Oh, yes. But on one condition."

Bartlett.—"Yes."

Constance.—"That you have a little faith in me, too."

Bartlett—"Oh, Miss Wyatt"—

Constance.—"I used to have a bad temper, and now that I'm getting better it seems to be getting worse. Try to believe in me enough to know that when I do or say some violent thing, I'm ashamed of it; and that when I wounded you, I really meant to hurt myself; that I—Oh, you know, Mr. Bartlett, how much you've borne from us, and how much we owe you; and if you did anything now to make us think less of your unselfish goodness, we never could forgive you!" Bartlett remains with bowed head. "I must go, now." Gaily : "Perhaps tomorrow, when we resume our lessons, you'll tell me what you meant to-day, when you couldn't explain yourself."

Bartlett, vehemently.—"No, I can never tell you."

Constance.—"I can't believe that! At any rate, we shall talk the matter over, and I may say something to help you. You know how one thing leads to another."

Bartlett—"But nothing you can ever say now will lead to what I wanted to say."

Constance, laughing.—"Don't be sure. If you rouse my curiosity, I shall be a powerful aid to expression. With a woman's wit to help you out with your meaning, how can you help making it clear? "

Bartlett.—"Because—because it wants something more than wit in you to make it clear."

Constance.—"Well, you shall have sympathy, if sympathy is what you need. Is it something like sympathy? "

Bartlett.—"Something like sympathy; but—not—not exactly sympathy."

Constance, with another laugh.—"How difficult you make it! I see! You want compassion."

Bartlett, quickly.—"Oh, no! I would sooner have contempt!"

Constance.—"But that's the one thing you can't have. Try to think of something else you want, and let me know to-morrow." She nods brightly to him, and he follows her going with a gaze of hopeless longing. As she vanishes through the doorway, he lifts his hand to his lips, and reverently kisses it to her.

Bartlett, alone.—"Try to think what I want and let you know! Ah, my darling, my darling! Your faith in me kills my hope. If you only dared a little less with me, how much more I might dare with you; and if you were not so sisterly sweet, how much sweeter you might be! Brother? Forty thousand brothers could not with all their quantity of love make up my sum! You drive me farther than your worst enemy from you with that fatal word. Brother? I hate brother! If it had been cousin— And kind? Oh, I would we were

'A little less than kin, and more than kind!

IV.
NOT AT ALL LIKE.

I.
BABTLETT and CUMMINGS.

Bartlett,—"Six weeks since you were here? I shouldn't have thought that." Bartlett's easel stands before the window, in the hotel parlour; he has laid a tint upon the canvas, and has retired a few paces for the effect, his palette and mahl-stick in hand, and his head carried at a critical angle. Cummings, who has been doing the duty of art-culture by the picture, regards it with renewed interest. Bartlett resumes his work : "Pretty good, Cummings?"

Cummings.—"Capital! The blue of that distance"—

Bartlett, with a burlesque sigh.—"Ah, I looked into my heart and painted for that! Well, you find me still here, Cummings, and apparently more at home than ever. The landlord has devoted this parlour to the cause of art,—makes the transients use the lower parlour, now,—and we have this all to ourselves : Miss Wyatt sketches, you know. Her mother brings her sewing, and the General his bruises; he hasn't quite scrambled up, yet, from that little knockdown of his; a man doesn't, at his time of life, I believe; and we make this our family-room; and a very queer family we are! Fine old fellow, the General; he's behaved himself since his accident like a disabled angel, and hasn't sworn,—well, anything worth sneaking of. Yes, here I am. I suppose it's all right, but for all I know it may be all wrong." Bartlett sighs in unguarded sincerity. "I don't know what I'm here for. Nature began shutting up shop a fortnight ago at a pretty lively rate, and edging loafers to the door, with every sign of impatience; and yet here I am, hanging round still. I suppose this glimpse of

Indian Summer is some excuse just now; it's a perfect blessing to the landlord, and he's making hay—rowen crop1—while the sun shines; I've been with him so long now, I take quite an interest in his prosperity, if eight dollars a week of it do come out of me! What is talked of in 'art-circles' down in Boston, brother Cummings?"

Cummings.—"Your picture."

Bartlett, inattentively, while he comes up to his canvas, and bestows an infinitesimal portion of paint upon a destitute spot in the canvas.—"Don't be sarcastic, Cummings."

Cummings.—"I'm not, I assure you."

Bartlett, turning toward him incredulously.—"Do you mean to say that The First Grey Hair is liked?"

Cummings.—"I do. There hasn't been any picture so much talked of this season."

Bartlett.—"Then it's the shameless slop of the name. I should think you'd blush for your part in that swindle. But clergymen have no conscience, where they've a chance to do a fellow a kindness, I've observed." He goes up to Cummings with his brush in his mouth, his palette on one hand, and his mahl-stick in the other, and contrives to lay hold of his shoulders with a few disengaged fingers. As Cummings shrinks a little from his embrace; "Oh, don't be afraid; I shan't get any paint on you. You need a whole coat of whitewash, though, you unscrupulous saint!" He returns to his easel. "So The Old Girl—that's what I shall call the picture—is a success, is she? The admiring public ought to see the original elm-tree now; she hasn't got a hair, grey or green, on her head; she's perfectly bald. I say, Cummings, how would it do for me to paint a pendant, The Last Grey Hair? I might look up a leaf or two on the elm, somewhere : stick it on to the point of twig; they wouldn't know any better."

Cummings.—"The leafless elm would make a good picture, whatever you called it." Bartlett throws back his shaggy head and laughs up at the ceiling. "The fact is, Bartlett, I've got a little surprise for you."

Bartlett, looking at him askance.—"Somebody wanting to chromo The Old Girl? No, no; it isn't quite so bad as that!"

Cummings, in a burst.—"They did want to chromo it. But it's sold. They've got you two hundred dollars for it." Bartlett lays down his brush, palette, and mahl-stick, dusts his fingers, puts them in his pockets, and comes and stands before Cummings, on whom, seated, he bends a curious look.

Bartlett.—"And do you mean to tell me, you hardened atheist, that you don't believe in the doctrine of future punishments? What are they going to do with you in the next world? And that picture-dealer? And me? Two hun—It's an outrage! It's—the picture wasn't worth fifty, by a stretch of the most charitable imagination! Two hundred d—Why, Cummings, I'll paint no end of Old Girls, First and Last Grey Hairs—I'll flood the market! Two—Good Lord!" Bartlett goes back to his easel, and silently resumes his work. After a while : "Who's been offered up?"

Cummings.—"What?"

Bartlett—"Who's the victim? My patron? The noble and discriminating and munificent purchaser of The Old Girl?"

Cummings.—"Oh! Mrs. Bellingham She's going to send it out to her daughter in Omaha."

Bartlett.—"Ah! Mrs. Blake wishes to found an art museum with that curiosity out there? Sorry for the Omaha-has." Cummings makes a gesture of impatience. "Well, well; I won't then, old fellow! I'm truly obliged to you. I accept my good fortune with compunction, but with all the gratitude imaginable. I say, Cummings!"

Cummings.—"Well?"

Bartlett—"What do you think of my taking to high art,—mountains twelve hundred feet above the sea, like this portrait of Ponkwasset?"

Cummings.—"I've always told you that you had only to give yourself scope,— attempt something worthy of your powers"—

Bartlett—"Ah, I thought so. Then you believe that a good big canvas and a good big subject would be the making of me? Well, I've come round to that idea myself. I used to think that if there was any greatness in me, I could get it into a small picture, like Meissonier or Corot. But I can't. I must have room, like the Yellowstone and Yo-Semite fellows. Don't you think Miss Wyatt is looking wonderfully improved?"

Cummings.—"Wonderfully! And how beautiful she is! She looked lovely that first day, in spite of her ghostliness; but now"—

Bartlett.—"Yes; a phantom of delight is good enough in its way, but a well woman is the prettiest, after all. Miss Wyatt sketches, I think I told you."

Cummings.—"Yes, you mentioned it."

Bartlett—"Of course. Otherwise, I couldn't possibly have thought of her while I was at work on a great picture like this, She sketches"—Bartlett puts his nose almost on the canvas in the process of bestowing a delicate touch—"she sketches about as badly as any woman I ever saw, and that's saying a good deal. But she looks uncommonly well while she's at it. The fact is, Cummings,"—Bartlett retires some feet from the canvas and squints at it,—"this very picture which you approve of so highly is—Miss Wyatt's. I couldn't attempt anything of the size of Ponkwasset! But she allows me to paint at it a little when she's away." Bartlett steals a look of joy at his friend's vexation, and then continues seriously : "I've been having a curious time, Cummings." The other remains silent "Don't you want to ask me about it?" Cummings.—"I don't know that I do." Bartlett—"Why, my dear old fellow, you're hurt! It was a silly joke, and I honestly ask your pardon." He lays down his brush and palette and leaves the easel. "Cummings, I don't know what to do. I'm in a perfect deuce of a state, I'm hit—awfully hard; and I don't know what to do about it. I wish I had gone at once—the first day. But I had to stay,—I had to stay." He turns and walks away from Cummings, whose eyes follow him in pardon and sympathy.

Cummings.—"Do you really mean it, Bartlett? I didn't dream of such a thing. I thought you were still brooding over that affair with Miss Harlan."

Bartlett—"Oh, child's-play! A prehistoric illusion! A solar myth! The thing never was." He rejects the obsolete superstition with a wave of his left hand. "I'm in love with this girl, and I feel like a sneak and a brute about it. At the very best it would be preposterous. Who am I, a poor devil of a painter, the particular pet of Poverty, to think of a young lady whose family and position could command her the best? But putting that aside,—putting that insuperable obstacle lightly aside, as a mere trifle,—the thing remains an atrocity. It's enormously indelicate to think of loving a woman who would never have looked twice at me if I hadn't resembled an infernal scoundrel who tried to break her heart; and I've nothing else to commend me. I've the perfect certainty that she doesn't and can't care anything for me in myself; and it grinds me into the dust to realise on what terms she tolerates me. I could carry it off as a joke at first; but when it became serious, I had to look it in the face; and that's what it amounts to, and if you know of any more hopeless and humiliating tangle, I don't." Bartlett, who has approached his friend during this speech, walks away again; and there is an interval of silence.

Cummings, at last, musingly.—"You in love with Miss Wyatt; I can't imagine it!"

Bartlett, fiercely.—"You can't imagine it? What's the reason you can't imagine it? Don't be offensive, Cummings!" He stops in his walk and lowers upon his friend. "Why shouldn't I be in love with Miss Wyatt?"

Cummings.—"Oh, nothing. Only you were saying—

Bartlett—"I was saying! Don't tell me what I was saying. Say something yourself."

Cummings.—"Really, Bartlett, you can't expect me to stand this sort of thing. You're preposterous."

Bartlett.—"I know it! But don't blame me. I beg your pardon. Is it because of the circumstances that you can't imagine my being in love with her?"

Cummings.—"Oh, no; I wasn't thinking of the circumstances; but it seemed so out of character for you"—

Bartlett, impatiently.—"Oh, love's always out of character, just as it's always out of reason. I admit freely that I'm an ass. And then?"

Cummings.—"Well, then, I don't believe you have any more reason to be in despair than you have to be in love. If she tolerates you, as you say, it can't be because you look like the man who jilted her."

Bartlett.—"Ah! But if she still loves him?"

Cummings.—"You don't know that. That strikes me as a craze of jealousy. What makes you think she tolerates you for that reason or no-reason?"

Bartlett.—"What makes me think it? From the very first she interpreted me by what she knew of him. She expected me to be this and not to be that; to have one habit and not another; and I could see that every time the fact was different, it was a miserable disappointment to her, a sort of shock. Every little difference between me and that other rascal gave her a start; and whenever I looked up I found her wistful eyes on me as if they were trying to puzzle me out; they used to follow me round the room like the eyes of a family portrait. You wouldn't have liked it yourself, Cummings. For the first three weeks I simply existed on false pretences,—involuntary false pretences, at that. I wanted to explode; I wanted to roar out. If you think I'm at all like that abandoned scoundrel of yours in anything but looks, I'm not! But

I was bound by everything that was decent, to hold my tongue, and let my soul be rasped out of me in silence and apparent unconsciousness. That was your fault. If you hadn't told me all about the thing, I could have done something outrageous and stopped it. But I was tied hand and foot by what I knew. I had to let it go on."

Cummings.—"I'm very sorry, Bartlett, but"—

Bartlett—"Oh, I dare say you wouldn't have done it if you hadn't had a wild ass of the desert to deal with. Well, the old people got used to some little individuality in me, by-and-by, and beyond a suppressed whoop or two from the mother when I came suddenly into the room, they didn't do anything to annoy me directly. But they were anxious every minute for the effect on her; and it worried me as much to have them watching her as to have her watching me. Of course I knew that she talked this confounded resemblance over with her mother every time I left them, and avoided talking it over with the father."

Ciimmings.—"But you say the trouble's over now."

Bartlett—"Oh—over! No, it isn't over. When she's with me a while she comes to see that I am not a mere doppelgänger. She respites me to that extent. But I have still some small rags of self-esteem dangling about me; and now suppose I should presume to set up for somebody on my own account; the first hint of my caring for her as I do, if she could conceive of anything so atrocious, would tear open all the old sorrows. Ah! I can't think of it. Besides, I tell you, it isn't all over. It's only not so bad as it was. She's subject to relapses, when it's much worse than ever. Why"— Bartlett stands facing his friend, with a half-whimsical, half-desperate smile, as if about to illustrate his point, when Constance and her mother enter the parlour.

II.
CONSTANCE, MRS. WYATT,
BABTLETT, and CUMMINGS.

Constance, with a quick violent arrest.—"Ah! Oh!"

Mrs. Wyatt—"Constance, Constance, darling! What's the matter?"

Constance.—"Oh, nothing—nothing." She laughs, nervously. "I thought there was nobody—here; and it—startled me. How do you do, Mr. Cummings?" She goes quickly up to that gentleman, and gives him her hand. "Don't you think it wonderful to find such a day as this, up here, at this time of year?" She struggles to control the panting breath in which she speaks.

Cummings.—"Yes, I supposed I had come quite too late for anything of the sort. You must make haste with your Ponkwasset, Miss Wyatt, or you'll have to paint him with his winter cap on."

Constance.—"Ah, yes! My picture. Mr. Bartlett has been telling you." Her eyes have already wandered away from Cummings, and they now dwell, with a furtive light of reparation and imploring upon Bartlett's disheartened patience; "Good morning." It is a delicately tentative salutation, in a low voice, still fluttered by her nervous agitation.

Bartlett, in dull despair: "Good morning."

Constance.—"How is the light on the mountain this morning?" She drifts deprecatingly up to the picture, near which Bartlett has stolidly kept his place.

Bartlett, in apathetic inattention.—"Oh, very well, very well indeed, thank you."

Constance, after a hesitating glance at him.—"Did you like what I had done on it yesterday?"

Bartlett, very much as before.—"Oh, yes; why not?"

Constance, with a meek subtlety.—"I was afraid I had vexed you—by it." She bends an appealing glance upon him, to which Bartlett remains impervious, and she drops her eyes with a faint sigh. Then she lifts them again : "I was afraid I had—made the distance too blue."

Bartlett.—"Oh, no; not at all."

Constance.—"Do you think I had better try to finish it?"

Bartlett.—"Oh, certainly. Why not? If it amuses you!"

Constance, perplexedly.—"Of course." Then with a sad significance : "But I know I am trying your patience too far. You have been so kind, so good, I can't forgive myself for annoying you."

Bartlett.—"It doesn't annoy me. I'm very glad to be useful to you."

Constance, demurely.—"I didn't mean painting; I meant—screaming." She lifts her eyes to Bartlett's face, with a pathetic, inquiring attempt at lightness, the slightest imaginable experimental archness in her self-reproach, which dies out as Bartlett frowns and bites the corner of his moustache in unresponsive silence. "I ought to be well enough now to stop it : I'm quite well enough to be ashamed of it." She breaks off a miserable little laugh.

Bartlett, with cold indifference.—"There's no reason why you should stop it—if it amuses you." She looks at him in surprise at this rudeness. "Do you wish to try your hand at Ponkwasset this morning?"

Constance, with a flash of resentment.—"No; thanks." Then with a lapse into her morbid self-abasement: "I shall not touch it again. Mamma!"

Mrs. Wyatt.—"Yes, Constance." Mrs. Wyatt and Cummings, both intent on Bartlett and Constance, have been heroically-feigning a polite interest in each other, from which pretence they now eagerly release themselves.

Constance.—"Oh—nothing. I can get it of Mary. I won't trouble you." She goes toward the door.

Mrs. Wyatt.—"Mary isn't up from her breakfast yet. If you want anything, let me go with you, dear." She turns to follow Constance. "Good morning, Mr. Cummings; we shall see you at dinner. Good morning,"—with an inquiring glance at Bartlett. Constance slightly inclines towards the two gentlemen without looking at them, in going out with her mother; and Cummings moves away to the piano, and affects to examine the sheet-music scattered over it. Bartlett remains in his place near the easel.

III.
BARTLETT and CUMMINGS.

Bartlett, harshly, after a certain silence which his friend is apparently resolved not to break.—"Sail in, Cummings!"

Cummings.—"Oh, I've got nothing to say."

Bartlett.—"Yes, you have. You think I'm a greater fool and a greater brute than you ever supposed in your most sanguine moments. Well, I am! What then?"

Cummings, turning about from the music at which he has been pretending to look, and facing Bartlett, with a slight shrug,—"If you choose to characterise your own behaviour in that way, I shall not dispute you at any rate."

Bartlett.—"Go on!"

Cummings.—"Go on? You saw yourself, I suppose, how she hung upon every syllable you spoke, every look, every gesture?"

Bartlett.—"Yes, I saw it."

Cummings.—"You saw how completely crushed she was by your tone and manner. You're not blind. Upon my word, Bartlett, if I didn't know what a good, kind-hearted fellow you are, I should say you were the greatest ruffian alive."

Bartlett, with a groan.—"Go on! That's something like."

Cummings.—"I couldn't hear what was going on—I'll own I tried—but I could see; and to see the delicate amende she was trying to offer you, in such a way that it should not seem an amende,—a perfect study of a woman's gracious, unconscious art,—and then to see your sour refusal of it all, it made me sick."

Bartlett, with a desperate clutch at his face, like a man oppressed with some stifling vapour.—"Yes, yes! I saw it all, too! And if it had been for me, I would have given anything for such happiness. Oh, gracious powers! How dear she is! I would rather have suffered any anguish than give her pain, and yet I gave her pain! I knew how it entered her heart : I felt it in my own. But what could I do? If I am to be my-self, if I am not to steal the tenderness meant for another man, the love she shows to me because I'm like somebody else, I must play the brute. But have a little mercy on me. At least, I'm a baited brute. I don't know which way to turn, I don't know what to do. She's so dear to me,—so dear in every tone of her voice, every look of her eyes, every aspiration or desire of her transparent soul, that it seems to me my whole being is nothing but a thought of her. I loved her helplessness, her pallor, her sorrow; judge how I adore her return to something like life! Oh, you blame me! You simplify this infernal perplexity of mine and label it brutality, and scold me for it. Great heaven! And yet you saw, you heard how she entered this room. In that instant the old illusion was back on her, and I was nothing. All that I had been striv-ing and longing to be to her, and hoping and despairing to seem, was swept out of existence; I was reduced to a body without a soul, to a shadow, a counterfeit! You think I resented it? Poor girl, I pitied her so; and my own heart all the time like lead in my breast,—a dull lump of ache! I swear, I wonder I don't go mad. I suppose—why, I suppose I am insane. No man in his senses was ever bedevilled by such a maniacal hallucination. Look here, Cummings : tell me that this damnable coil isn't simply a matter of my own fancy. It'll be some little relief to know that it's real."

Cummings,—"It's real enough, my dear fellow. And it is a trial,—more than I could have believed such a fantastic thing could be."

Bartlett—"Trial? Ordeal by fire! Torment! I can't stand it any longer."

Cummings, musingly.—"She is beautiful, isn't she, with that faint dawn of red in her cheeks,—not a colour, but a coloured light like the light that hangs round a rose-tree's boughs in the early spring! And what a magnificent movement, what a stately grace! The girl must have been a goddess!"

Bartlett—"And now she's a saint—for sweetness and patience! You think she's had nothing to suffer before from me? You know me better! Well, I'm going away."

Cummings.—"Perhaps it will be the best. You can go back with me to-mor-row."

Bartlett—"To-morrow? Go back with you to-morrow? What are you talking about, man?" Cummings smiles. "I can't go to-morrow. I can't leave her hating me."

Cummings.—"I knew you never meant to go. Well, what will you do?"

Bartlett.—"Don't be so cold-blooded! What would you do?"

Cummings.—"I would have it out somehow."

Bartlett.—"Oh, you talk! How?"

Cummings.—"I am not in love with Miss Wyatt"

Bartlett—"Oh, don't try to play the cynic with me! It doesn't become you. I know I've used you badly at times, Cummings. I behaved abominably in leaving you to take the brunt of meeting General Wyatt that first day; I said so then, and I shall always say it. But I thought you had forgiven that."

Cummings, with a laugh.—"You make it hard to treat you seriously, Bartlett. What do you want me to do? Do you want me to go to Miss Wyatt and explain your case to her?"

Bartlett, angrily.—"No!"

Cummings.—"Perhaps to Mrs. Wyatt?"

Bartlett, infuriate.—"No!"

Cummings.—"To the General?"

Bartlett, with sudden quiet.—"You had better go away from here, Cummings—while you can."

Cummings.—"I see you don't wish me to do anything, and you're quite right. Nobody can do anything but yourself."

Bartlett.—"And what would you advise me to do?"

Cummings.—"I've told you that I would have it out. You can't make matters worse. You can't go on in this way indefinitely. It's just possible that you might find yourself mistaken,—that Miss Wyatt cares for you in your own proper identity."

Bartlett—"For shame!"

Cummings.—"Oh, if you like!"

Bartlett, after a pause.—"Would you—would you see the General?"

Cummings.—"If I wanted to marry the General. Come, Bartlett; don't be ridiculous. You know you don't want my advice, and I haven't any to give, I must go to my room a moment."

Bartlett—"Well, go! You're of no advantage here. You'd have it out, would you? Well, then, I wouldn't I'm a brute, I know, and a fool, but I'm not such brute and fool as that!" Cummings listens with smiling patience, and then goes without reply, while Bartlett drops into the chair near the easel, and sulkily glares at the picture. Through the window at his back shows the mellow Indian summer landscape. The trees have all dropped their leaves, save the oaks which show their dark crimson banners among the deep green of the pines and hemlocks on the hills; the meadows, verdant as in June, slope away toward the fringe of birches and young maples along the borders of the pond; the low-blackberry trails like a running fire over the long grass limp from the first frosts, which have silenced all the insect voices. No sound of sylvan life is heard but the harsh challenge of a jay, answered from many trees of the nearest wood-lot. The far-off hill-tops are molten in the soft azure haze of the season; the nearer slopes and crests sleep under a greyer and thinner veil. It is to this scene that the painter turns from the easel, with the sullen unconsciousness in which he has dwelt upon the picture. Its beauty seems at last to penetrate his mood; he rises and looks upon it; then he goes out on the gallery, and, hidden by the fall of one of the curtains, stands leaning upon the rail and rapt in the common reverie of the dreaming world. While he lingers there, Cummings appears at the door, and looks in; then with an air of some surprise, as if wondering not to see Bartlett, vanishes again, to give place to General Wyatt, who after a like research retires silently and apparently disconcerted. A few moments later Mrs. Wyatt comes to the threshold, and calling gently into the room, "Constance!" waits briefly and goes away. At last, the young girl herself appears, and falters in the doorway an instant, but finally comes forward and drifts softly and indirectly up to the picture, at which she glances with a little sigh. At the same moment Bartlett's voice, trolling a snatch of song, comes from the gallery without:—

ROMANCE.
I.

Here apart our paths, then, lie: This way you wend, that way I; Speak one word before you go : Do not, do not leave me so I

II.

What is it that I should say? Tell me quick; I cannot stay; Quick! I am not good at guessing: Night is near, and time is pressing.

III.

Nay, then, go! But were I you, I will tell you what I'd do: Bather than be baffled so, I would never, never go!

As the song ends, Bartlett reappears at the gallery door giving into the parlour, and encounters Constance turning at his tread from the picture on which she has been pensively gazing while he sang. He puts up a hand on either side of the door.

IV.
BARTLETT and CONSTANCE.

Bartlett.—"I didn't know you were here."

Constance.—"Neither did I—know you were, till I heard you singing."

Bartlett, smiling ironically.—"Oh, you didn't suppose I sang!"

Constance, confusedly.—"I—I don't know"—

Bartlett—"Ah, you thought I did! I don't. I was indulging in a sort of modulated howling which I flatter myself is at least one peculiarity that's entirely my own. I was baying the landscape merely for my private amusement, and I'd not have done it, if I'd known you were in hearing. However, if it's helped to settle the fact one way or other, concerning any little idiosyncrasy of mine, I shan't regret it. I hope not to disappoint you in anything, by-and-by." He drops his hands from the door-posts and steps into the room, while Constance, in shrinking abeyance, stands trembling at his harshness.

Constance, in faltering reproach.—"Mr. Bartlett!"

Bartlett—"Constance!"

Constance, struggling to assert herself, but breaking feebly in her attempt at hauteur.—"Constance? What does this mean, Mr. Bartlett?"

Bartlett, with a sudden burst.—"What does it mean? It means that I'm sick of this nightmare masquerade. It means that I want to be something to you—all the world to you—in and for myself. It means that I can't play another man's part any longer and live. It means that I love you, love you, love you, Constance!" He starts involuntarily toward her with outstretched arms, from which she recoils with a convulsive cry.

Constance.—"You love me? Me? Oh, no, no! How can you be so merciless as to talk to me of love?" She drops her glowing face into her hands.

Bartlett.—"Because I'm a man. Because love is more than mercy—better, higher, wiser. Listen to me, Constance!—yes, I will call you so now if never again : you are so dear to me that I must say it at last if it killed you. If loving you is cruel, I'm pitiless! Give me some hope, tell me to breathe, my girl!"

Constance.—"Oh go, while I can still forgive you."

Bartlett—"I won't go; I won't have your forgiveness; I will have all or nothing; I want your love!"

Constance, uncovering her face and turning its desolation upon him; "My love? I have no love to give. My heart is dead."

Bartlett.—"No, no! That's part of the ugly trance that we've both been living in so long. Look! You're better now than when you came here; you're stronger, braver, more beautiful. My angel, you're turned a woman again! Oh, you can love me if you will; and you will! Look at me, darling!" He takes her listless right hand in his left, and gently draws her toward him.

Constance, starting away.—"You're wrong; you're all wrong! You don't understand; you don't know—Oh, listen to me!"

Bartlett, still holding her cold hand fast.—"Yes, a thousand years. But you must tell me first that I may love you. That first!"

Constance.—"No! That never! And since you speak to me of love, listen to what it's my right you should hear."

Bartlett, releasing her.—"I don't care to hear. Nothing can ever change me. But if you bid me, I will go!"

Constance.—"You shall not go now till you know what despised and hated and forsaken thing you've offered your love to."

Bartlett, beseechingly.—"Constance, let me go while I can forgive myself. Nothing you can say will make me love you less; remember that; but I implore you to spare yourself. Don't speak, my love."

Constance.—"Spare myself? Not speak? Not speak what has been on my tongue and heart and brain, a burning fire, so long?—Oh, I was a happy girl once! The days were not long enough for my happiness; I woke at night to think of it. I was proud in my happiness and believed myself, poor fool, one to favour those I smiled on; and I had my vain and crazy dreams of being the happiness of some one who should come to ask for—what you ask now. Some one came. At first I didn't care for him, but he knew how to make me. He knew how to make my thoughts of him part of my happiness and pride and vanity till he was all in all, and I had no wish, no hope, no life but him; and then he—left me!" She buries her face in her hands again, and breaks into a low, piteous sobbing.

Bartlett, with a groan of helpless fury and compassion.—"The fool, the sot, the slave! Constance, I knew all this,—I knew it from the first."

Constance, recoiling in wild reproach.—"You knew it?"

Bartlett, desperately,—"Yes, I knew it—in spite of myself, through my own stubborn fury I knew it, that first day, when I had obliged my friend to tell me what your father had told him, before I would hear reason. I would have given anything not to have known it then, when it was too late, for I had at least the grace to feel the wrong, the outrage of my knowing it. You can never pardon it, I see; but you must feel what a hateful burden I had to bear, when I found that I had somehow purloined the presence, the looks, the voice of another man—a man whom I would have joyfully changed myself to any monstrous shape not to resemble, though I knew that my likeness to him, bewildering you in a continual dream of him, was all that ever made you look at me or think of me. I lived in the hope—Heaven only knows why I should have had the hope!—that I might yet be myself to you; that you might wake from your dream of him and look on me in the daylight, and see that I was at least an honest man, and pity me and may be love me at last, as I loved you at first, from the moment I saw your dear pale face, and heard your dear, sad voice." He follows up her slow retreat and again possesses himself of her hand : "Don't cast me off! It was monstrous, out of all decency, to know your sorrow; but I never tried to know it; I tried not to know it." He keeps fast hold of her hand, while she remains with averted head. "I love you, Constance; I loved you; and when once you had bidden me stay, I was helpless to go away, or I would never be here now to offend you with the confession of that shameful knowledge. Do you think it was no trial to me? It gave me the conscience of an eavesdropper and a spy; yet all I knew was sacred to me."

Constance, turning and looking steadfastly into his face.—"And you could care for so poor a creature as I—so abject, so obtuse as never to know what had made her intolerable to the man that cast her off?"

Bartlett—"Man? He was no man! He"—

Constance, suddenly.—"Oh, wait! I—I love him yet."

Bartlett, dropping her hand.—"You"—

Constance.—"Yes, yes! As much as I live, I love him! But when he left me, I seemed to die; and now it's as if I were some wretched ghost clinging for all existence to the thought of my lost happiness. If that slips from me, then I cease to be."

Bartlett.—"Why, this is still your dream. But I won't despair. You'll wake yet, and care for me : I know you will."

Constance, tenderly.—"Oh, I'm not dreaming now. I know that you are not he. You are everything that is kind and good; and some day you will be very happy."

Bartlett, desolately.—"I shall never be happy without your love." After a pause : "It will be a barren, bitter comfort, but let me have it if you can : if I had met you first, could you have loved me?"

Constance.—"I might have loved you if—I had—lived." She turns from him again, and moves softly toward the door; his hollow voice arrests her.

Bartlett—"If you are dead, then I have lived too long. Your loss takes the smile out of life for me." A moment later : "You are cruel, Constance."

Constance, abruptly facing him.—"I cruel? To you?"

Bartlett.—"Yes, you have put me to shame before myself. You might have spared me! A treacherous villain is false in time to save you from a life of betrayal, and you say your heart is dead. But that isn't enough. You tell me that you cannot care for me because you love that treacherous villain still. That's my disgrace, that's my humiliation, that's my killing shame. I could have borne all else. You might have cast me off however you would, driven me away with any scorn, whipped me from you with the sharpest rebuke that such presumption as mine could merit; but to drag a decent man's self-respect through such mire as that poor rascal's memory for six long weeks, and then tell him that you prefer the mire"—

Constance.—"Oh, hush! I can't let you reproach him! He was pitilessly false to me, but I will be true to him for ever. How do I know—I must find some reason for that, or there is no reason in anything!—how do I know that he did not break his word to me at my father's bidding? My father never liked him."

Bartlett, shaking his head with a melancholy smile.—"Ah, Constance, do you think I would break my word to you at your father's biddmg?"

Constance, in abject despair.—"Well, then I go back to what I always knew; I was too slight, too foolish, too tiresome for his life-long love. He saw it in time, I don't blame him. You would see it, too."

Bartlett.—"What devils vantage enabled that infernal scoundrel to blight your spirit with his treason? Constance, is this my last answer?"

Constance.—"Yes, go! I am so sorry for you,—sorrier than I ever thought I could be for anything again."

Bartlett.—"Then if you pity me, give me a little hope that sometime, some-how"—

Constance.—"Oh, I have no hope, for you, for me, for any one. Good-bye, good, kind friend! Try,—you won't have to try hard—to forget me. Unless some miracle should happen to show me that it was all his fault and none of mine, we are parting now for ever. It has been a strange dream, and nothing is so strange as that it should be ending so. Are you the ghost or I, I wonder! It confuses me as it did at first; but if you are he, or only you—Ah, don't look at me so, or I must believe he has never left me, and implore you to stay!"

Bartlett, quietly—"Thanks. I would not stay a moment longer in his disguise, if you begged me on your knees. I shall always love you, Constance, but if the world is wide enough, please Heaven, I will never see you again. There are some things dearer to me than your presence. No, I won't take your hand; it can't heal the hurt your words have made, and nothing can help me, now I know from your own lips that but for my likeness to him I should never have been anything to you. Good-bye!"

Constance.—"Oh!" She sinks with a long cry into the arm-chair beside the table, and drops her head into her arms upon it. At the door toward which he turns Bartlett meets General Wyatt, and a moment later Mrs. Wyatt enters by the other. Bartlett recoils under the concentrated reproach and inquiry of their gaze.

V.
GENERAL WYATT, MRS. WYATT, CONSTANCE, and BARTLETT.

Mrs. Wyatt, hastening to bow herself over Constance's fallen head.—"Oh, what is it, Constance?" As Constance makes no reply, she lifts her eyes again to Bartlett's face.

General Wyatt, peremptorily.—"Well, sir!"

Bartlett, with bitter desperation.—"Oh, you shall know!"

Constance, interposing.—"I will tell! You shall be spared that, at least." She has risen, and with her face still hidden in her handkerchief, seeks her father with an outstretched hand. He tenderly gathers her to his arms, and she droops a moment upon his shoulder; then, with an electrical revolt against her own weakness, she lifts her head and dries her tears with a passionate energy. "He—Oh, speak for me!" Her head falls again on her father's shoulder.

Bartlett, with grave irony and self-scorn.—"It's a simple matter, sir; I have been telling Miss Wyatt that I love her, and offering to share with her my obscurity and poverty. I"—

General Wyatt, impatiently.—"Curse your poverty, sir! I'm poor myself. Well !"

Bartlett—"Oh, that's merely the beginning; I have had the indecency to do this knowing that what alone rendered me sufferable to her it was a cruel shame for me to know, and an atrocity for me to presume upon. I"—

General Wyatt.—"I authorised this knowledge on your part when I spoke to your friend, and before he went away he told me all he had said to you,"

Bartlett, in the first stages of petrifaction.—"Cummings?"

General Wyatt.—"Yes."

Bartlett.—"Told you that I knew whom I was like?"

General Wyatt—"Yes."

Bartlett, very gently.—"Then I think that man will be lost for keeping his conscience too clean. Cummings has invented a new sin."

Mrs. Wyatt.—"James, James! You told me that Mr. Bartlett didn't know."

General Wyatt, contritely.—"I let you think so, Margaret; I didn't know what else to do."

Mrs. Wyatt.—"Oh, James!"

Constance.—"Oh, papa!" She turns with bowed head from her father's arms, and takes refuge in her mother's embrace. General Wyatt, released, fetches a compass round about the parlour, with a face of intense dismay. He pauses in front of his wife.

General Wyatt.—"Margaret, you must know the worst now."

Mrs. Wyatt, in gentle reproach, while she softly caresses Constance's hair.— "Oh, is there anything worse, James?"

General Wyatt, hopelessly.—"Yes; I'm afraid I have been to blame."

Bartlett.—"General Wyatt, let me retire. I"—

General Wyatt.—"No, sir. This concerns you, too, now. Your destiny has entangled you with our sad fortunes, and now you must know them all."

Constance, from her mother's shoulder.—"Yes, stay,—whatever it is. If you care for me, nothing can hurt you any more, now."

General Wyatt—"Margaret,—Constance! If I have been mistaken in what I have done, you must try somehow to forgive me; it was my tenderness for you both misled me, if I erred. Sir, let me address my defence to you. You can see the whole matter with clearer eyes than we." At an imploring gesture from Bartlett, he turns again to Mrs. Wyatt. "Perhaps you are right, sir. Margaret, when I had made up my mind that the wretch who had stolen our child's heart was utterly unfit and unworthy"—

Constance, starting away from her mother with a cry.—"Ah, you did drive him from me then! I knew, I knew it! And after all these days and weeks and months that seem years and centuries of agony, you tell me that it was you broke my heart! No, no, I never will forgive you, father! Where is he? Tell me that! Where is my husband—the husband you robbed me of? Did you kill him, when you chose to crush my life? Is he dead? If he's living I will find him wherever he is. No distance and no danger shall keep me from him. I'll find him and fall down before him, and implore him to forgive you, for I never can! Was this your tenderness for me—to drive him away, and leave me to the pitiless humiliation of believing myself deserted? Oh, great tenderness!"

General Wyatt, confronting her storm with perfect quiet.—"No, I will give better proof of my tenderness than that." He takes from his pocket-book a folded paper which he hands to his wife : "Margaret, do you know that writing?"

Mrs. Wyatt, glancing at the superscription.—"Oh, too well! This is to you, James."

General Wyatt.—"It's for you now. Read it."

Mrs. Wyàtt, wonderingly unfolding the pàper and then reading.—"'I confess myself guilty of forging Major Cummings's signature, and in consideration of his and your own forbearance, I promise never to see Miss Wyatt again. I shall always be grateful for your mercy; and'—James, James! It isn't possible!"

Constance, who has crept nearer and nearer while her mother has been reading, as if drawn by a resistless fascination.—"No, it isn't possible! It's false; it's a fraud! I will see it," She swiftly possesses herself of the paper and scans the handwriting for a moment with a fierce intentness. Then she flings it wildly away. "Yes, yes, it's true! It's his hand. It's true, it's the only true thing in this world of lies!" She totters away toward the sofa. Bartlett makes a movement to support her, but she repulses him, and throws herself upon the cushions.

General Wyatt.—"Sir, I am sorry to make you the victim of a scene. It has been your fate, and no part of my intention. Will you look at this paper? You don't know all that is in it yet." He touches it with his foot.

Bartlett, in dull dejection.—"No, I won't look at it. If it were a radiant message from heaven, I don't see how it could help me now."

Mrs. Wyatt.—"I'm afraid you've made a terrible mistake, James."

General Wyatt.—"Margaret! Don't say that!"

Mrs. Wyatt.—"Yes, it would have been better to show us this paper at once,—better than to keep us all these days in this terrible suffering."

General Wyatt—"I was afraid of greater suffering for you both, I chose sorrow for Constance rather than the ignominy of knowing that she had set her heart on so base a scoundrel. When he crawled in the dust there before me, and whined for pity, I revolted from telling you or her how vile he was; the thought of it seemed to dishonour you; and I had hoped something, everything, from my girl's self-respect, her obedience, her faith in me. I never dreamed that it must come to this."

Mrs. Wyatt, sadly shaking her head.—"I know how well you meant; but oh, it was a fatal mistake!"

Constance, abandoning her refuge among the cushions, and coming forward to her father,—"No, mother, it was no mistake! I see now how wise and kind and merciful you have been, papa. You can never love me again, I've behaved so badly; but if you'll let me, I will try to live my gratitude for your mercy at a time when the whole truth would have killed me. Oh, papa! What shall I say, what shall I do to show how sorry and ashamed I am? Let me go down on my knees to thank you." Her father catches her to his heart, and fondly kisses her again and again. "I don't deserve it, papa! You ought to hate me, and drive me from you, and never let me see you again." She starts away from him as if to execute upon herself this terrible doom, when her eye falls upon the letter where she had thrown it on the floor. "To think how long I have been the fool, the slave of that—felon!" She stoops upon the paper with a hawk-like fierceness; she tears it into shreds, and strews the fragments about the room." Oh, if I could only tear out of my heart all thoughts of him, all memory, all likeness!" In her wild scorn she has whirled unheedingly away toward Bartlett, whom, suddenly confronting, she apparently addresses in this aspiration; he opens wide his folded arms.

Bartlett—"And what would you do, then, with this extraordinary resemblance?" The closing circle of his arms involves her and clasps her to his heart, from which beneficent shelter she presently exiles herself a pace or two, and stands with either hand pressed against his breast while her eyes dwell with rapture on his face.

Constance.—"Oh, you're not like him, and you never were!"

Bartlett, with light irony : "Ah?"

Constance.—"If I had not been blind, blind, blind, I never could have seen the slightest similarity. Like him? Never!"

Bartlett.—"Ah! Then perhaps the re-semblance, which we have noticed from time to time, and which has been the cause of some annoyance and embarrassment all round, was simply a disguise which I had assumed for the time being to accomplish a purpose of my own?"

Constance.—"Oh, don't jest it away! It's your soul that I see now, your true and brave and generous heart; and if you pardoned me for mistaking you a single moment for one who had neither soul nor heart, I could never look you in the face again!"

Bartlett—"You seem to be taking a good provisional glare at me beforehand, then, Miss Wyatt. I've never been so nearly looked out of countenance in my life. But you needn't be afraid; I shall not pardon your crime." Constance abruptly drops her head upon his breast, and again instantly repels herself.

Constance.—"No, you must not if you could. But you can't—you can't care for me after hearing what I could say to my father"—

Bartlett.—"That was in a moment of great excitement."

Constance.—"After hearing me rave about a man so unworthy of—any one—you cared for. No, your self-respect—everything—demands that you should cast me off."

Bartlett.—"It does. But I am inexorable,—you must have observed the trait before. In this case I will not yield even to my own colossal self-respect." Earnestly : "Ah, Constance, do you think I could love you the less because your heart was too true to swerve even from a traitor till he was proved as false to honour as to you?" Lightly again : "Come, I like your fidelity to worthless people; I'm rather a deep and darkling villain myself."

Constance, devoutly.—"You? Oh, you are as nobly frank and open as—as—as papa!"

Bartlett.—"No, Constance, you are wrong, for once. Hear my dreadful secret; I'm not what I seem,—the light and joyous creature I look,—I'm an emotional wreck. Three short years ago, I was frightfully jilted"—they all turn upon him in surprise—"by a young person who, I'm sorry to say, hasn't yet consoled me by turning out a scamp."

Constance, drifting to his side with a radiant smile.—"Oh, I'm so glad."

Bartlett, with affected dryness.—"Are you? I didn't know it was such a laughing matter. I was always disposed to take those things seriously."

Constance.—"Yes, yes! But don't you see? It places us on more of an equality."

She looks at him with a smile of rapture and logic exquisitely compact.

Bartlett.—"Does it? But you're not half as happy as I am."

Constance.—"Oh yes, I am! Twice."

Bartlett.—"Then that makes us just even, for so am I." They stand ridiculously blest, holding each other's hand a moment, and then Constance, still clinging to one of his hands, goes and rests her other arm upon her mother's shoulder.

Constance.—"Mamma, how wretched I have made you, all these months!"

Mrs. Wyatt.—"If your trouble's over now, my child,"—she tenderly kisses her cheek,—"there's no trouble for your mother in the world."

Constance.—"But I'm not happy, mamma. I can't be happy, thinking how wickedly unhappy I've been. No, no! I had better go back to the old wretched state again; it's all I'm fit for. I'm so ashamed of myself. Send him away!" She renews her hold upon his hand.

Bartlett.—"Nothing of the kind. I was requested to remain here six weeks ago, by a young lady. Besides, this is a public house. Come, I haven't finished the catalogue of my disagreeable qualities yet. I'm jealous. I want you to put that arm on my shoulder." He gently effects the desired transfer, and then, chancing to look up, he discovers the Rev. Arthur Cummings on the threshold in the act of modestly retreating. He detains him with a great melodramatic start. "Hah! A clergyman! This is indeed ominous!"

THE PARLOUR CAR.
A FARCE.

SCENE : A Parlour Car on the New York Central Railroad. It is late afternoon in the early autumn, with a cloudy sunset threatening rain. The car is unoccupied save by a gentleman, who sits fronting one of the windows, with his feet in another chair; a newspaper lies across his lap; his hat is drawn down over his eyes, and he is apparently asleep. The rear door of the car opens, and the conductor enters with a young lady, heavily veiled, the porter coming after with her wraps and travelling-bags. The lady's air is of mingled anxiety and desperation, with a certain fierceness of movement She casts a careless glance over the empty chairs.

Conductor.—"Here's your ticket, madam. You can have any of the places you like here, or,"—glancing at the unconscious gentleman, and then at the young lady—"if you prefer, you can go and take that seat in the forward car,"

Miss Lucy Galbraith.—"Oh, I can't ride backwards. I'll stay here, please. Thank you." The porter places her things in a chair by a window, across the car from the sleeping gentleman, and she throws herself wearily into the next seat, wheels round in it, and lifting her veil gazes absently out at the landscape. Her face, which is very pretty, with a low forehead shadowed by thick, blonde hair, shows the traces of tears. She makes search in her pocket for her handkerchief, which she presses to her eyes. The conductor, lingering a moment, goes out.

Porter.—"I'll be right here, at de end of de cah, if you should happen to want anything, miss,"—making a feint of arranging the shawls and satchels. "Should you like some dese things hung up? Well, dey'll be jus' as well in de chair. We's pretty late dis afternoon; more'n four hours behin' time. Ought to been into Albany 'fore dis. Freight train off de track jus' dis side o' Rochester, an' had to wait. Was you goin' to stop at Schenectady, miss?"

Miss G., absently.—"At Schenectady?" After a pause, "Yes."

Porter.—"Well, that's de next station, and den de cahs don't stop ag'in till dey git to Albany. Anything else I can do for you now, miss?"

Miss G.—"No, no, thank you, nothing." The porter hesitates, takes off his cap, and scratches his head with a murmur of embarrassment. Miss Galbraith looks up at him inquiringly, and then suddenly takes out her porte-monnaie and fees him.

Porter.—"Thank you, miss, thank you. If you want anything at all, miss, I'm right dere at de end of de cah." He goes out by the narrow passage-way beside the smaller enclosed parlour. Miss Galbraith looks askance at the sleeping gentleman, and then, rising, goes to the large mirror, to pin her veil, which has become loosened from her hat. She gives a little start at sight of the gentleman in the mirror, but arranges her headgear, and returning to her place looks out of the window again. After a little while she moves about uneasily in her chair, then leans forward and tries to raise her window j she lifts it partly up, when the catch slips from her fingers and the window falls shut again with a crash.

Miss G.—"O dear, how provoking! I suppose I must call the porter," She rises from her seat, but on attempting to move away she finds that the skirt of her polonaise has been caught in the falling window. She pulls at it, and then tries to lift the window again, but the cloth has wedged it in, and she cannot stir it. "Well, I certainly think this is beyond endurance! Porter! Ah—porter! Oh, he'll never hear me in the racket that these wheels are making! I wish they'd stop—I"—

The gentleman stirs in his chair, lifts his head, listens, takes his feet down from the other seat, rises abruptly, and comes to Miss Galbraith's side.

Mr. Allen Richards.—"Will you allow me to open the window for you?" Starting back, "Miss Galbraith!"

Miss G.—"A1—Mr. Richards!" There is a silence for some moments, in which they remain looking at each other; then,

Mr. Richards.—"Lucy"—

Miss G.—"I forbid you to address me in that way, Mr, Richards."

Mr. R.—"Why, you were just going to call me Allen!"

Miss G.—"That was an accident, you know very well—an impulse"

Mr. R.—"Well, so is this."

Miss G.—"Of which you ought to be ashamed to take advantage. I wonder at your presumption in speaking to me at all. It's quite idle, I can assure you. Everything is at an end between us. It seems that I bore with you too long; but I'm thankful that I had the spirit to act at last, and to act in time. And now that chance has thrown us together, I trust that you will not force your conversation upon me. No gentleman would, and I have always given you credit for thinking yourself a gentleman. I request that you will not speak to me."

Mr. R.—"You've spoken ten words to me for every one of mine to you. But I won't annoy you. I can't believe it, Lucy; I can not believe it. It seems like some rascally dream, and if I had had any sleep since it happened, I should think I had dreamed it."

Miss G.—"Oh! You were sleeping soundly enough when I got into the car!"

Mr. R.—"I own it; I was perfectly used up, and I had dropped off."

Miss G., scornfully.—"Then perhaps you have dreamed it."

Mr. R.—"I'll think so till you tell me again that our engagement is broken; that the faithful love of years is to go for nothing; that you dismiss me with cruel insult, without one word of explanation, without a word of intelligible accusation, even. It's too much I've been thinking it all over and over, and I can't make head or tail of it. I meant to see you again as soon as we got to town, arid implore you to hear me. Come, it's a mighty serious matter, Lucy, I'm not a man to put on heroics and that; but I believe it'll play the very deuce with me, Lucy,—that is to say, Miss Galbraith,—I do indeed. It'll give me a low opinion of woman."

Miss G., averting her face.—"Oh, a very high opinion of woman you have had!"

Mr. R., with sentiment.—"Well, there was one woman whom I thought a perfect angel."

Miss G.—"Indeed I May I ask her name?"

Mr. R., with a forlorn smile.—"I shall be obliged to describe her somewhat formally as—Miss Galbraith."

Miss G.—"Mr. Richards!"

Mr. R.—"Why, you've just forbidden toe to say Lucy. You must tell me, dearest, what I have done to offend you. The worst criminals are not condemned unheard, and I've always thought you were merciful if not just. And now I only ask you to be just."

Miss G., looking out of the window.—"You know very well what you've done. You can't expect me to humiliate myself by putting your offence into words."

Mr. R.—"Upon my soul, I don't know what you mean! I don't know what I've done. When you came at me, last night, with my ring and presents and other little traps, you might have knocked me down with the lightest of the lot. I was perfectly dazed; I couldn't say anything before you were off, and all I could do was to hope that you'd be more like yourself in the morning. And in the morning, when I came round to Mrs. Phillips's I found you were gone, and I came after you by the next train."

Miss G.—"Mr. Richards, your personal history for the last twenty-four hours is a matter of perfect indifference to me, as it shall be for the next twenty-four hundred years. I see that you are resolved to annoy me, and since you will not leave the car, I must do so." She rises haughtily from her seat, but the imprisoned skirt of her polonaise twitches her abruptly back into her chair. She bursts into tears. "Oh, what shall I do!"

Mr. B., dryly.—"You shall do whatever you like, Miss Galbraith, when I've set you free; for I see your dress is caught in the window. When it's once out, I'll shut the window, and you can call the porter to raise it." He leans forward over her chair, and while she shrinks back the length of her tether, he tugs at the window-fastening. "I can't get at it. Would you be so good as to stand up,—all you can?" Miss Galbraith stands up, droopingly, and Mr. Richards makes a movement towards her, and then falls back. "No, that won't do. Please sit down again." He goes round her chair and tries to get at the window from that side. "I can't get any purchase on it. Why don't you cut out that piece?" Miss Galbraith stares at him in dumb amazement. "Well, I don't see what we're to do. I'll go and get the porter." He goes to the end of the car, and returns. "I can't find the porter—he must be in one of the other cars. But"—brightening with the fortunate conception—"I've just thought of something. Will it unbutton?"

Miss G.—"Unbutton?"

Mr. R.—"Yes; this garment of yours."

Miss G.—"My polonaise?" Inquiringly: "Yes."

Mr. R.—"Well, then, it's a very simple matter. If you will just take it off I can easily"—

Miss G., faintly.—"I can't. A polonaise isn't like an overcoat"—

Mr. R., with dismay.—"Oh! Well, then"—He remains thinking a moment in hopeless perplexity.

Miss G., with polite ceremony.—"The porter will be back soon. Don't trouble yourself any further about it, please. I shall do very well."

Mr. G., without heeding her,—"If you could kneel on that foot-cushion and face the window"—

Miss G., kneeling promptly.—"So?'

Mr. R—"Yes, and now"—kneeling beside her—"if you'll allow me to—to get at the window catch,"—he stretches both arms forward; she shrinks from his right into his left, and then back again,—"and pull, while I raise the window"—

Miss G.—"Yes, yes; but do hurry, please. If any one saw us, I don't know what they would think. It's perfectly ridiculous!"—pulling. "It's caught in the corner of the window, between the frame and the sash, and it won't come! Is my hair troubling you? Is it in your eyes?"

Mr. R.—"It's in my eyes, but it isn't troubling me. Am I inconveniencing you?"

Mr. G.—"Oh, not at all."

Mr. R.—"Well, now then, pull hard!" He lifts the window with a great effort; the polonaise comes, free with a start, and she strikes violently against him. In supporting the shock he cannot forbear catching her for an instant to his heart. She frees herself, and starts indignantly to her feet.

Miss G.—"Oh, what a cowardly—subterfuge!"

Mr. R.—"Cowardly? You've no idea how much courage it took." Miss Galbraith puts her handkerchief to her face and sobs. "Oh, don't cry! Bless my heart—I'm sorry I did it! But you know how dearly I love you, Lucy, though I do think you've been cruelly unjust. I told you I never should love anyone else, and I never shall. I couldn't help it, upon my soul I couldn't. Nobody could. Don't let it vex you, my"—He approaches her.

Miss G.—"Please not touch me, sir! You have no longer any right whatever to do so."

Mr. R.—"You misinterpret a very inoffensive gesture. I have no idea of touching you, but I hope I may be allowed, as a special favour, to—pick up my hat, which you are in the act of stepping on." Miss Galbraith hastily turns, and strikes the hat with her whirling skirts; it rolls to the other side of the parlour, and Mr. Richards, who goes after it, utters an ironical "Thanks!" He brushes it and puts it on, looking at her where she has again seated herself at the window with her back to him, and continues, "As for any further molestation from me"—

Miss G.—"If you will talk to me"—

Mr. R.—"Excuse me, I am not talking to you."

Miss G.—"What were you doing?"

Mr. R.—"I was beginning to think aloud. I—I was soliloquising. I suppose I may be allowed to soliloquise?"

Miss G., very coldly.—"You can do what you like."

Mr. R.—"Unfortunately that's just what I can't do. If I could do as I liked, I should ask you a single question."

Miss G., after a moment.—"Well, sir, you may ask your question." She remains as before, with her chin in her hand, looking tearfully out of the window; her face is turned from Mr. Richards, who hesitates a moment, before he speaks.

Mr. R.—"I wish to ask you just this, Miss Galbraith: if you couldn't ride backwards in the other car, why do you ride backwards in this?"

Miss G., burying her face in her handkerchief, and sobbing.—"Oh, oh, oh! This is too bad!"

Mr. R.—"Oh, come now, Lucy. It breaks my heart to hear you going on so, and all for nothing. Be a little merciful to both of us, and listen to me. I've no doubt I can explain everything if I once understand it, but it's pretty hard explaining a thing if you don't understand it yourself. Do turn round. I know it makes you sick to ride in that way, and if you don't want to face me—there!"—wheeling in his chair so as to turn his back upon her—"you needn't. Though it's rather trying to a fellow's politeness, not to mention his other feelings. Now, what in the name"—

Porter, who at this moment enters with his step-ladder, and begins to light the lamps.—"Going pretty slow ag'in, sah."

Mr. R.—"Yes; what's the trouble?"

Porter.—"Well, I don't know exactly, sah. Something de matter with de loco-motive. We shan't be into Albany much 'fore eight o'clock."

Mr. R.—"What's the next station?"

Porter.—"Schenectady."

Mr. R.—"Is the whole train as empty as this car?"

Porter, laughing.—"Well, no, sah. Fact is, dis cah don't belong on dis train. It's a Pullman that we hitched on when you got in, and we's taking it along for one of de Eastern roads. We let you in 'cause de Drawing-rooms was all full. Same with de lady"—looking sympathetically at her, as he takes up his steps to go out. "Can I do anything for you now, miss?"

Miss G., plaintively.—"No, thank you; nothing whatever." She has turned while Mr. Richards and the porter have been speaking, and now faces the back of the former, but her veil is drawn closely. The porter goes out.

Mr. R., wheeling round so as to confront her.—"I wish you would speak to me half as kindly as you do to that darky, Lucy."

Miss G.—"He is a gentleman!" Mr. R.—"He is an urbane and well-informed nobleman. At any rate, he's a man and a brother. But so am I." Miss Galbraith does not reply, and after a pause Mr. Richards resumes. "Talking of gentlemen : I recollect, once, coming up on the day-boat to Poughkeepsie, there was a poor devil of a tipsy man kept following a young fellow about, and annoying him to death—trying to fight him, as a tipsy man will, and insisting that the young fellow had insulted him. By-and-by he lost his balance, and went overboard, and the other jumped after him and fished him out." Sensation on the part of Miss Galbraith, who stirs uneasily in her chair, looks out of the window, then looks at Mr. Richards, and drops her head. "There was a young lady on board, who had seen the whole thing—a very charming young lady indeed, with pale blonde hair growing very thick over her forehead, and dark eyelashes to the sweetest blue eyes in the world. Well, this young lady's papa was amongst those who came up to say civil things to the young fellow when he got aboard again, and to ask the honour—he said the honour—of his acquaintance. And when he came out of his state-room in dry clothes, this infatuated old gentleman was waiting for him, and took him and introduced him to his wife and daughter. And the daughter said, with tears in her eyes, and a perfectly intoxicating impulsiveness, that it was the grandest and the most heroic and the noblest thing that she had ever seen, and she should always be a better girl for having seen it Excuse me, Miss Galbraith, for troubling you with these facts of a personal history which, as you say, is a matter of perfect indifference to you. The young fellow didn't think at the time he had done anything extraordinary; but I don't suppose he did expect to live to have the same girl tell him he was no gentleman."

Miss G., wildly.—"Oh, Allen, Allen! You know I think you are a gentleman, and I always did!"

Mr. R., languidly.—"Oh, I merely had your word for it, just now, that you didn't.'

Tenderly.—"Will you hear me, Lucy?"

Miss G., faintly.—"Yes."

Mr. JR.—"Well, what is it I've done? Will you tell me if I guess right?"

Miss G., with dignity,—"I am in no humour for jesting, Allen. And I can assure you that though I consent to hear what you have to say, or ask, nothing will change my determination. All is over between us."

Mr. R.—"Yes, I understand that perfectly. I am now asking merely for general information. I do not expect you to relent, and in fact I should consider it rather frivolous if you did. No. What I have always admired in your character, Lucy, is a firm, logical consistency; a clearness of mental vision that leaves no side of a subject unsearched; and an unwavering constancy of purpose. You may say that these traits are characteristic of all women; but they are pre-eminently characteristic of you, Lucy." Miss Gal-braith looks askance at him, to make out whether he is in earnest or not; he continues, with a perfectly serious air. "And I know now that if you're offended with me, it's for no trivial cause." She stirs uncomfortably in her chair. "What I have done I can't imagine, but it must be something monstrous, since it has made life with me appear so impossible that you are ready to fling away your own happiness—for I know you did love me, Lucy—and destroy mine. I will begin with the worst thing I can think of. Was it because I danced so much with Fanny Watervliet?"

Miss G., indignantly.—"How can you insult me by supposing that I could be jealous of such a perfect little goose as that? No, Allen! Whatever I think of you, I still respect you too much for that."

Mr. R.—"I'm glad to hear that there are yet depths to which you think me incapable of descending, and that Miss Watervliet is one of them. I will now take a little higher ground. Perhaps you think I flirted with Mrs. Dawes. I thought, myself, that the thing might begin to have that appearance, but I give you my word of honour that as soon as the idea occurred to me, I dropped her,—rather rudely, too. The trouble was, don't you know, that I felt so perfectly safe with a married friend of yours. I couldn't be hanging about you all the time, and I was afraid I might vex you if I went with the other girls; and I didn't know what to do."

Miss G.—"I think you behaved rather silly, giggling so much with her. But"—

Mr. R.—"I own it, I know it was silly. But"—

Miss G.—"It Wasn't that; it wasn't that!"

Mr. R.—"Was it my forgetting to bring you those things from your mother?"

Miss G.—"No!"

Mr. R.—"Was it because I hadn't given up smoking yet?"

Miss G.—"You know I never asked you to give up smoking. It was entirely your own proposition."

Mr. R.—"That's true. That's what made me so easy about it. I knew I could leave it off any time. Well, I will not disturb you any longer, Miss Galbraith." He throws his overcoat across his arm, and takes up his travelling-bag. "I have failed to guess your fatal—conundrum; and I have no longer any excuse for remaining. I am going into the smoking-car. Shall I send the porter to you for anything?"

Miss G.—"No, thanks." She puts up her handkerchief to her face.

Mr. R.—"Lucy, do you send me away?"

Miss G., behind her handkerchief.—"You were going, yourself."

Mr. R., over his shoulder.—"Shall I come back?"

Miss G.—"I have no right to drive you from the car."

Mr. R., coming back, and sitting down in the chair nearest her.—"Lucy, dearest, tell me what's the matter."

Miss G.—"Oh, Allen, your not knowing makes it all the more hopeless and killing. It shows me that we must part; that you would go on, breaking my heart, and grinding me into the dust as long as we lived." She sobs, "It shows me that you never understood me, and you never will. I know you're good and kind and all that, but that only makes your not understanding me so much the worse. I do it quite as much for your sake as my own, Allen."

Mr. R.—"I'd much rather you wouldn't put yourself out on my account."

Miss G., without regarding him.—"If you could mortify me before a whole roomful of people as you did last night, what could I expect after marriage but continual insult?"

Mr. R., in amazement.—"How did I mortify you? I thought that I treated you with all the tenderness and affection that a decent regard for the feelings of others would allow. I was ashamed to find I couldn't keep away from you."

Miss G.—"O, you were attentive enough, Allen; nobody denies that. Attentive enough in non-essentials. O yes!"

Mr. R.—"Well, what vital matters did I fail in? I'm sure I can't remember."

Miss G.—"I dare say! I dare say they won't appear vital to you, Allen. Nothing does. And if I had told you, I should have been met with ridicule, I suppose. But I knew better than to tell; I respected myself too much."

Mr. R.—"But now you mustn't respect yourself quite so much, dearest. And I promise you I won't laugh at the most serious thing, I'm in no humour for it. If it were a matter of life and death, even, I can assure you that it wouldn't bring a smile to my countenance. No, indeed! If you expect me to laugh, now, you must say something particularly funny."

Miss G.—"I was not going to say anything funny, as you call it, and I will say nothing at all, if you talk in that way."

Mr. R.—"Well, I won't, then. But do you know what I suspect, Lucy? I wouldn't mention it to everybody, but I will to you—in strict confidence : I suspect that you're rather ashamed of your grievance, if you have any. I suspect it's nothing at all."

Miss G., very sternly at first, with a rising hysterical inflection,—"Nothing, Allen! Do you call it nothing, to have Mrs. Dawes come out with all that about your accident on your way up the river, and ask me if it didn't frighten me terribly to hear of it, even after it was all over; and I had to say you hadn't told me a word of it? 'Why, Lucy!'"—angrily mimicking Mrs. Dawes—"'you must teach him better than that. I make Mr. Dawes tell me everything.' Little simpleton! And then to have them all laugh—oh dear, it's too much!"

Mr. R.—"Why, my dear Lucy—"

Miss G., interrupting him.—"I saw just how it was going to be, and I'm thankful, thankful that it happened. I saw that you didn't care enough for me to take me into your whole life; that you despised and distrusted me, and that it would get worse and worse to the end of our days; that we should grow further and further apart, and I should be left moping at home, while you ran about making confidantes of other women whom you considered worthy of your confidence. It all flashed upon me in an instant; and I resolved to break with you, then and there; and I did, just as soon as ever I could go to my room for your things, and I'm glad,—yes,—O hu, hu, hu, hu, hu!—so glad I did it!"

Mr. R., grimly.—"Your joy is obvious. May I ask—"

Miss G.—"Oh, it wasn't the first proof you had given me how little you really cared for me, but I was determined it should be the last. I dare say you've forgotten them! I dare say you don't remember telling Mamie Morris that you didn't like crocheted cigar-cases, when you'd just told me that you did, and let me be such a fool as to commence one for you; but I'm thankful to say that went into the fire,—O yes, instantly! And I dare say you've forgotten that you didn't tell me your brother's engagement was to be kept, and let me come out with it that night at the Rudges' and then looked perfectly aghast, so that everybody thought I had been blabbing! Time and again, Allen, you have made me suffer agonies, yes, agonies; but your power to do so is at an end, I am free and happy at last." She weeps bitterly.

Mr. R., quietly.—"Yes, I had forgotten those crimes, and I suppose many similar atrocities. I own it, I am forgetful and careless. I was wrong about those things. I ought to have told you why I said that to Miss Morris; I was afraid she was going to work me one. As to that accident I told Mrs, Dawes of, it wasn't worth mentioning. Our boat simply walked over a sloop in the night, and nobody was hurt. I shouldn't have thought twice about it, if she hadn't happened to brag of their passing close to an iceberg on their way home from Europe; then I trotted out my pretty-near disaster as a match for hers,—confound her! I wish the iceberg had sunk them! Only it wouldn't have sunk her,—she's so light! She'd have gone bobbing all over the Atlantic Ocean, like a cork; she's got a perfect life-preserver in that mind of hers." Miss Galbraith gives a little laugh, and then a little moan. "But since you are happy, I will not repine, Miss Galbraith. I don't pretend to be very happy myself, but then, I don't deserve it. Since you are ready to let an absolutely unconscious offence on my part cancel all the past; since you let my devoted love weigh as nothing against the momentary pique that a malicious little rattle-pate—she was vexed at my leaving her—could make you feel, and choose to gratify a wicked resentment at the cost of any suffering to me, why, I can be glad and happy, too." With rising anger, "Yes, Miss Galbraith. All is over between us. You can go! I renounce you!"

Miss G., springing fiercely to her feet.—"Go, indeed! Renounce me! Be so good as to remember that you haven't got me to renounce!"

Mr. R.—"Well, it's all the same thing. I'd renounce you if I had. Good evening, Miss Galbraith. I will send back your presents as soon as I get to town; it won't be necessary to acknowledge them. I hope we may never meet again." He goes out of the door towards the front of the car, but returns directly, and glances uneasily at Miss Galbraith, who remains with her handkerchief pressed to her eyes. "Ah—a—that is—I shall be obliged to intrude upon you again. The fact is—"

Miss G., anxiously.—"Why, the cars have stopped! Are we at Schenectady?"

Mr. R.—"Well, no; not exactly; not exactly at Schenectady"—

Miss G.—"Then what station is this? Have they carried me by? Observing his embarrassment, "Allen, what is the matter? What has happened? Tell me instantly! Are we off the track? Have we run into another train? Have we broken through a bridge? Shall we be burnt alive? Tell me, Allen, tell me,—I can bear it!—are we telescoped?" She wrings her hands in terror.

Mr. R., unsympathetically.—"Nothing of the kind has happened. This car has simply come uncoupled, and the rest of the train has gone on ahead, and left us standing on the track nowhere in particular." He leans back in his chair, and wheels it round from her.

Miss G., mortified, yet anxious.—"Well?"

Mr. R.—"Well, until they miss us, and run back to pick us up, I shall be obliged to ask your indulgence. I will try not to disturb you; I would go out and stand on the platform, but it's raining."

Miss G., listening to the rain-fall on the roof.—"Why, so it is!" Timidly, "Did you notice when the car stopped?"

Mr. R.—"No." He rises and goes out at the rear door, comes back, and sits down again.

Miss G. rises and goes to the large mirror to wipe away her tears. She glances at Mr. Richards, who does not move. She sits down in a seat nearer him than the chair she has left. After some faint murmurs and hesitations, she asks, "Will you please tell me why you went out just now?"

Mr. R., with indifference.—"Yes. I went to see if the rear signal was out."

Miss G., after another hesitation.—"Why?"

Mr. R.—"Because, if it wasn't out, some train might run into us from that direction."

Miss G., tremulously.—"Oh! And was it?"

Mr. R., dryly.—"Yes."

Miss G. returns to her former place with a wounded air, and for a moment neither speaks. Finally she asks very meekly, "And there's no danger from the front?"

Mr. R., coldly.—"No."

Miss G., after some little noises and movements meant to catch Mr. R.'s attention.—"Of course, I never meant to imply that you were intentionally careless or forgetful."

Mr. R., still very coldly.—"Thank you."

Miss G.—"I always did justice to your good-heartedness, Allen; you're perfectly lovely that way; and I know that you would be sorry if you knew you had wounded my feelings, however accidentally." She droops her head so as to catch a sidelong glimpse of his face, and sighs, while she nervously pinches the top of her parasol, resting the point on the floor. Mr. R. makes no answer. "That about the cigar-case might have been a mistake; I saw that myself, and, as you explain it, why, it was certainly very kind and very creditable to—to your thoughtfulness. It was thoughtful!"

Mr. R.—"I am grateful for your good opinion."

Miss G.—"But do you think it was exactly—it was quite—nice, not to tell me that your brother's engagement was to be kept, when you know, Allen, I can't bear to blunder in such things?" Tenderly, "Do you? You can't say it was?"

Mr. R.—"I never said it was."

Miss G., plaintively.—"No, Allen. That's what I always admired in your character. You always owned up. Don't you think it's easier for men to own up than it is for women?"

Mr. R.—"I don't know. I never knew any woman to do it."

Miss G.—"O yes, Allen! You know I often own up."

Mr. R.—"No, I don't."

Miss G.—"Oh, how can you bear to say so? When I'm rash, or anything of that kind, you know I acknowledge it."

Mr. R.—"Do you acknowledge it now?"

Miss G.—"Why, how can I, when I haven't been rash? What have I been rash about?"

Mr. R.—"About the cigar-case, for example."

Miss G.—"Oh! That! That was a great while ago! I thought you meant something quite recent," A sound as of the approaching train is heard in the distance. She gives a start, and then leaves her chair again for one a little nearer his. "I thought perhaps you meant about—last night."

Mr. R,—"Well?"

Miss G., very judicially.—"I don't think it was rash exactly. No, not rash. It might not have been very kind not to—to—trust you more, when I knew that you didn't mean anything; but—No, I took the only course I could. Nobody could have done differently under the circumstances. But if I caused you any pain, I'm very sorry; O yes, very sorry indeed. But I was not precipitate, and I know I did right. At least I tried to act for the best. Don't you believe I did?"

Mr. R.—"Why, if you have no doubt upon the subject, my opinion is of no consequence."

Miss G.—"Yes. But what do you think? If you think differently, and can make me see it differently, oughtn't you to do so?"

Mr. R,—"I don't see why. As you say, all is over between us."

Miss G.—"Yes." After a pause, "I should suppose you would care enough for yourself to wish me to look at the matter from the right point of view."

Mr. R.—"I don't."

Miss G., becoming more and more uneasy as the noise of the approaching train grows louder.—"I think you have been very quick with me at times, quite as quick as I could have been with you last night." The noise is more distinctly heard. "I'm sure that if I could once see it as you do, no one would be more willing to do anything in their power to atone for their rashness. Of course I know that everything is over."

Mr. R.—"As to that, I have your word; and, in view of the fact, perhaps this analysis of motive, of character, however interesting on general grounds, is a little"—

Miss G., with sudden violence.—"Say it, and take your revenge! I have put myself at your feet, and you do right to trample on me! O, this is what women may expect when they trust to men's generosity! Well, it is over now, and I'm thankful, thankful! Cruel, supicious, vindictive, you're all alike, and I'm glad that I'm no longer subject to your heartless caprices. And I don't care what happens after this, I shall always—Oh! You're sure it's from the front, Allen? Are you sure the rear signal is out?"

Mr. R., relenting.—"Yes, but if it will ease your mind, I'll go and look again." He rises and starts towards the rear door.

Miss G., quickly.—"O no! Don't go! I can't bear to be left alone! "The sound of the approaching train continually increases in volume. "O, isn't it coming very, very, very fast?"

Mr. R.—"No, no! Don't be frightened."

Miss G., running towards the rear door.—"O, I must get out! It will kill me, I know it will. Come with me! Do, do!" He runs after her, and her voice is heard at the rear of the car. "O, the outside door is locked, and we are trapped, trapped, trapped! O, quick! Let's try the door at the other end." They re-enter the parlour, and the roar of the train announces that it is upon them. "No, no! It's too late, it's too late! I'm a wicked, wicked girl, and this is all to punish me! O, it's coming, it's coming at full speed!" He remains bewildered, confronting her. She utters a wild cry, and, as the train strikes the car with a violent concussion, she flings herself into his arms. "There, there! Forgive me, Allen! Let us die together, my own, own love!" She hangs fainting on his breast. Voices are heard without, and after a little delay the porter comes in with a lantern.

Porter.—"Rather more of a jah than we meant to give you, sah! We had to run down pretty quick after we missed you, and the rain made the track a little slippery. Lady much frightened?"

Miss G., disengaging herself.—"O, not at all! Not in the least. We thought it was a train coming from behind, and going to run into us, and so—we—I—"

Porter.—"Not quite so bad as that. We'll be into Schenectady in a few minutes, miss. I'll come for your things." He goes out at the other door.

Miss G., in a fearful whisper.—"Allen! What will he ever think of us? I'm sure he saw us!"

Mr. R.—"I don't know what he'll think now. He did think you were frightened; but you told him you were not. However, it isn't important what he thinks. Probably he thinks I'm your long lost brother. It had a kind of familiar look."

Miss G.—"Ridiculous!"

Mr. R.—"Why, he'd never suppose that I was a jilted lover of yours!"

Miss G., ruefully.—"No."

Mr. R.—"Come, Lucy,"—taking her hand,—"you wished to die with me, a moment ago. Don't you think you can make one more effort to live with me? I won't take advantage of words spoken in mortal peril, but I suppose you were in earnest when you called me your own—own—" Her head droops; he folds her in his arms, a moment, then she starts away from him, as if something had suddenly occurred to her.

Miss G.—"Allen, where are you going?"

Mr. R.—"Going? Upon my soul, I haven't the least idea."

Miss G.—"Where were you going?"

Mr. R.—"O, I was going to Albany."

Miss G.—"Well, don't! Aunt Mary is expecting me here at Schenectady,—I telegraphed her,—and I want you to stop here, too, and we'll refer the whole matter to her. She's such a wise old head. I'm not sure"—

Mr. R.—"What?"

Miss G., demurely.—"That I'm good enough for you."

Mr. R., starting, in burlesque of her movement, as if a thought had struck him.—"Lucy! how came you on this train when you left Syracuse on the morning express?"

Miss G., faintly,—"I waited over a train at Utica." She sinks into a chair and averts her face.

Mr. R.—"May I ask why?"

Miss G., more faintly still.—"I don't like to tell. I"—

Mr. R., coming and standing in front of her, with his hands in his pockets.—"Look me in the eye, Lucy!" She drops her veil over her face, and looks up at him. "Did you—did you expect to find me on this train?"

Miss G.—"I was afraid it never would get along,—it was so late!"

Mr. R.—"Don't—tergiversate."

Miss G.—"Don't what?"

Mr. R.—"Fib."

Miss G.—"Not for worlds!"

Mr. R.—"How did you know I was in this car?"

Miss G.—"Must I? I thought I saw you through the window; and then I made sure it was you when I went to pin my veil on,—I saw you in the mirror."

Mr. R., after a little silence.—"Miss Galbraith, do you want to know what you are?"

Miss G., softly.—"Yes, Allen"

Mr. R.—"You're a humbug!"

Miss G., springing from her seat, and confronting him.—"So are you! You pretended to be asleep!"

Mr. R.—"I—I—I was taken by surprise. I had to take time to think."

Miss G.—"So did I."

Mr. R.—"And you thought it would be a good plan to get your polonaise caught in the window?"

Miss G., hiding her face on his shoulder.—"No, no, Allen! That I never will admit. No woman would!"

Mr. R.—"O, I dare say!" After a pause : "Well, I am a poor, weak, helpless man, with no one to advise me or counsel me, and I have been cruelly deceived. How could you, Lucy, how could you? I can never get over this." He drops his head upon her shoulder.

Miss G., starting away again and looking about the car.—"Allen, I have an idea! Do you suppose Mr. Pullman could be induced to sell this car?"

Mr. R.—"Why?"

Miss G.—"Why, because I think it's perfectly lovely, and I should like to live in it always. It could be fitted up for a sort of summer-house, don't you know, and we could have it in the garden, and you could smoke in it."

Mr. R.—"Admirable! It would look just like a travelling photographic saloon. No, Lucy, we won't buy it; we will simply keep it as a precious souvenir, a sacred memory, a beautiful dream,—and let it go on fulfilling its destiny all the same."

Porter, entering and gathering up Miss Galbraith's things.—"Be at Schenectady in half a minute, miss. Won't have much time."

Miss G., rising and adjusting her dress, and then looking about the car, while she passes her hand through her lover's arm.—"O, I do hate to leave it. Farewell, you dear, kind, good, lovely car! May you never have another accident!" She kisses her hand to the car, upon which they both look back as they slowly leave it.

Mr. R., kissing his hand in like manner.—"Good-bye, sweet chariot! May you never carry any but bridal couples I"

Miss G.—"Or engaged ones!"

Mr. R.—"Or husbands going home to their wives!"

Miss G.—"Or wives hastening to their husbands."

Mr. R.—"Or young ladies who have waited one train over, so as to be with the young men they hate."

Miss G.—"Or young men who are so indifferent that they pretend to be asleep when the young ladies come in!" They pause at the door and look back again. "'And must I leave thee, Paradise?'" They both kiss their hands to the car again, and their faces being very close together, they impulsively kiss each other. Then Miss Galbraith throws back her head, and solemnly confronts him. "Only think, Allen! If this car hadn't broken its engagement, we might never have mended ours."

The Codes Of Hammurabi And Moses
W. W. Davies

QTY

The discovery of the Hammurabi Code is one of the greatest achievements of archaeology, and is of para- mount interest, not only to the student of the Bible, but also to all those interested in ancient history...

Religion   **ISBN:** *1-59462-338-4*   **Pages:132**

MSRP $12.95

The Theory of Moral Sentiments
Adam Smith

QTY

This work from 1749. contains original theories of con- science amd moral judgment and it is the foundation for systemof morals.

Philosophy **ISBN:** *1-59462-777-0*   **Pages:536**

MSRP $19.95

Jessica's First Prayer
Hesba Stretton

QTY

In a screened and secluded corner of one of the many railway-bridges which span the streets of London there could be seen a few years ago, from five o'clock every morning until half past eight, a tidily set-out coffee-stall, consisting of a trestle and board, upon which stood two large tin cans, with a small fire of charcoal burning under each so as to keep the coffee boiling during the early hours of the morning when the work-people were thronging into the city on their way to their daily toil...

Pages:84

Childrens   **ISBN:** *1-59462-373-2*   *MSRP $9.95*

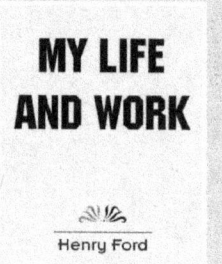

My Life and Work
Henry Ford

QTY

Henry Ford revolutionized the world with his implementation of mass production for the Model T automobile. Gain valuable business insight into his life and work with his own auto-biography... "We have only started on our development of our country we have not as yet, with all our talk of wonderful progress, done more than scratch the surface. The progress has been wonderful enough but..."

Pages:300

Biographies/   **ISBN:** *1-59462-198-5*   *MSRP $21.95*

The Art of Cross-Examination
Francis Wellman

QTY

I presume it is the experience of every author, after his first book is published upon an important subject, to be almost overwhelmed with a wealth of ideas and illustrations which could readily have been included in his book, and which to his own mind, at least, seem to make a second edition inevitable. Such certainly was the case with me; and when the first edition had reached its sixth impression in five months, I rejoiced to learn that it seemed to my publishers that the book had met with a sufficiently favorable reception to justify a second and considerably enlarged edition. ...

Pages:412

Reference   ISBN: *1-59462-647-2*   *MSRP $19.95*

On the Duty of Civil Disobedience
Henry David Thoreau

QTY

Thoreau wrote his famous essay, On the Duty of Civil Disobedience, as a protest against an unjust but popular war and the immoral but popular institution of slave-owning. He did more than write—he declined to pay his taxes, and was hauled off to gaol in consequence. Who can say how much this refusal of his hastened the end of the war and of slavery ?

Law   ISBN: *1-59462-747-9*   **Pages:48**
                                       MSRP $7.45

Dream Psychology Psychoanalysis for Beginners
Sigmund Freud

QTY

Sigmund Freud, born Sigismund Schlomo Freud (May 6, 1856 - September 23, 1939), was a Jewish-Austrian neurologist and psychiatrist who co-founded the psychoanalytic school of psychology. Freud is best known for his theories of the unconscious mind, especially involving the mechanism of repression; his redefinition of sexual desire as mobile and directed towards a wide variety of objects; and his therapeutic techniques, especially his understanding of transference in the therapeutic relationship and the presumed value of dreams as sources of insight into unconscious desires.

Pages:196

Psychology   ISBN: *1-59462-905-6*   *MSRP $15.45*

The Miracle of Right Thought
Orison Swett Marden

QTY

Believe with all of your heart that you will do what you were made to do. When the mind has once formed the habit of holding cheerful, happy, prosperous pictures, it will not be easy to form the opposite habit. It does not matter how improbable or how far away this realization may see, or how dark the prospects may be, if we visualize them as best we can, as vividly as possible, hold tenaciously to them and vigorously struggle to attain them, they will gradually become actualized, realized in the life. But a desire, a longing without endeavor, a yearning abandoned or held indifferently will vanish without realization.

Pages:360

Self Help   ISBN: *1-59462-644-8*   *MSRP $25.45*

The Rosicrucian Cosmo-Conception Mystic Christianity by *Max Heindel* ISBN: *1-59462-188-8* **$38.95**
The Rosicrucian Cosmo-conception is not dogmatic, neither does it appeal to any other authority than the reason of the student. It is: not controversial, but is: sent forth in the, hope that it may help to clear... New Age/Religion Pages 646

Abandonment To Divine Providence by *Jean-Pierre de Caussade* ISBN: *1-59462-228-0* **$25.95**
"The Rev. Jean Pierre de Caussade was one of the most remarkable spiritual writers of the Society of Jesus in France in the 18th Century. His death took place at Toulouse in 1751. His works have gone through many editions and have been republished... Inspirational/Religion Pages 400

Mental Chemistry by *Charles Haanel* ISBN: *1-59462-192-6* **$23.95**
Mental Chemistry allows the change of material conditions by combining and appropriately utilizing the power of the mind. Much like applied chemistry creates something new and unique out of careful combinations of chemicals the mastery of mental chemistry... New Age Pages 354

The Letters of Robert Browning and Elizabeth Barret Barrett 1845-1846 vol II ISBN: *1-59462-193-4* **$35.95**
by *Robert Browning* and *Elizabeth Barrett* Biographies Pages 596

Gleanings In Genesis (volume I) by *Arthur W. Pink* ISBN: *1-59462-130-6* **$27.45**
Appropriately has Genesis been termed "the seed plot of the Bible" for in it we have, in germ form, almost all of the great doctrines which are afterwards fully developed in the books of Scripture which follow... Religion/Inspirational Pages 420

The Master Key by *L. W. de Laurence* ISBN: *1-59462-001-6* **$30.95**
In no branch of human knowledge has there been a more lively increase of the spirit of research during the past few years than in the study of Psychology, Concentration and Mental Discipline. The requests for authentic lessons in Thought Control, Mental Discipline and... New Age/Business Pages 422

The Lesser Key Of Solomon Goetia by *L. W. de Laurence* ISBN: *1-59462-092-X* **$9.95**
This translation of the first book of the "Lernegton" which is now for the first time made accessible to students of Talismanic Magic was done, after careful collation and edition, from numerous Ancient Manuscripts in Hebrew, Latin, and French... New Age/Occult Pages 92

Rubaiyat Of Omar Khayyam by *Edward Fitzgerald* ISBN: *1-59462-332-5* **$13.95**
Edward Fitzgerald, whom the world has already learned, in spite of his own efforts to remain within the shadow of anonymity, to look upon as one of the rarest poets of the century, was born at Bredfield, in Suffolk, on the 31st of March, 1809. He was the third son of John Purcell... Music Pages 172

Ancient Law by *Henry Maine* ISBN: *1-59462-128-4* **$29.95**
The chief object of the following pages is to indicate some of the earliest ideas of mankind, as they are reflected in Ancient Law, and to point out the relation of those ideas to modern thought. Religion/History Pages 452

Far-Away Stories by *William J. Locke* ISBN: *1-59462-129-2* **$19.45**
"Good wine needs no bush, but a collection of mixed vintages does. And this book is just such a collection. Some of the stories I do not want to remain buried for ever in the museum files of dead magazine-numbers an author's not unpardonable vanity..." Fiction Pages 272

Life of David Crockett by *David Crockett* ISBN: *1-59462-250-7* **$27.45**
"Colonel David Crockett was one of the most remarkable men of the times in which he lived. Born in humble life, but gifted with a strong will, an indomitable courage, and unremitting perseverance... Biographies/New Age Pages 424

Lip-Reading by *Edward Nitchie* ISBN: *1-59462-206-X* **$25.95**
Edward B. Nitchie, founder of the New York School for the Hard of Hearing, now the Nitchie School of Lip-Reading, Inc, wrote "LIP-READING Principles and Practice". The development and perfecting of this meritorious work on lip-reading was an undertaking... How-to Pages 400

A Handbook of Suggestive Therapeutics, Applied Hypnotism, Psychic Science ISBN: *1-59462-214-0* **$24.95**
by *Henry Munro* Health/New Age/Health/Self-help Pages 376

A Doll's House: and Two Other Plays by *Henrik Ibsen* ISBN: *1-59462-112-8* **$19.95**
Henrik Ibsen created this classic when in revolutionary 1848 Rome. Introducing some striking concepts in playwriting for the realist genre, this play has been studied the world over. Fiction/Classics/Plays 308

The Light of Asia by *sir Edwin Arnold* ISBN: *1-59462-204-3* **$13.95**
In this poetic masterpiece, Edwin Arnold describes the life and teachings of Buddha. The man who was to become known as Buddha to the world was born as Prince Gautama of India but he rejected the worldly riches and abandoned the reigns of power when... Religion/History/Biographies Pages 170

The Complete Works of Guy de Maupassant by *Guy de Maupassant* ISBN: *1-59462-157-8* **$16.95**
"For days and days, nights and nights, I had dreamed of that first kiss which was to consecrate our engagement, and I knew not on what spot I should put my lips..." Fiction/Classics Pages 240

The Art of Cross-Examination by *Francis L. Wellman* ISBN: *1-59462-309-0* **$26.95**
Written by a renowned trial lawyer, Wellman imparts his experience and uses case studies to explain how to use psychology to extract desired information through questioning. How-to/Science/Reference Pages 408

Answered or Unanswered? by *Louisa Vaughan* ISBN: *1-59462-248-5* **$10.95**
Miracles of Faith in China Religion Pages 112

The Edinburgh Lectures on Mental Science (1909) by *Thomas* ISBN: *1-59462-008-3* **$11.95**
This book contains the substance of a course of lectures recently given by the writer in the Queen Street Hall, Edinburgh. Its purpose is to indicate the Natural Principles governing the relation between Mental Action and Material Conditions... New Age/Psychology Pages 148

Ayesha by *H. Rider Haggard* ISBN: *1-59462-301-5* **$24.95**
Verily and indeed it is the unexpected that happens! Probably if there was one person upon the earth from whom the Editor of this, and of a certain previous history, did not expect to hear again... Classics Pages 380

Ayala's Angel by *Anthony Trollope* ISBN: *1-59462-352-X* **$29.95**
The two girls were both pretty, but Lucy who was twenty-one who supposed to be simple and comparatively unattractive, whereas Ayala was credited, as her Bombwhat romantic name might show, with poetic charm, and a taste for romance. Ayala when her father died was nineteen... Fiction Pages 484

The American Commonwealth by *James Bryce* ISBN: *1-59462-286-8* **$34.45**
An interpretation of American democratic political theory. It examines political mechanics and society from the perspective of Scotsman James Bryce Politics Pages 572

Stories of the Pilgrims by *Margaret P. Pumphrey* ISBN: *1-59462-116-0* **$17.95**
This book explores pilgrims religious oppression in England as well as their escape to Holland and eventual crossing to America on the Mayflower, and their early days in New England... History Pages 268

QTY

The Fasting Cure by *Sinclair Upton*　　　　　　　　　　　　　ISBN: *1-59462-222-1*　**$13.95**
*In the Cosmopolitan Magazine for May, 1910, and in the Contemporary Review (London) for April, 1910, I published an article dealing with my experi-
ences in fasting. I have written a great many magazine articles, but never one which attracted so much attention...* New Age/Self Help/Health Pages 164

Hebrew Astrology by *Sepharial*　　　　　　　　　　　　　　ISBN: *1-59462-308-2*　**$13.45**
*In these days of advanced thinking it is a matter of common observation that we have left many of the old landmarks behind and that we are now pressing
forward to greater heights and to a wider horizon than that which represented the mind-content of our progenitors...*　　　　Astrology Pages 144

Thought Vibration or The Law of Attraction in the Thought World　　ISBN: *1-59462-127-6*　**$12.95**

by *William Walker Atkinson*　　　　　　　　　　　　　　　　Psychology/Religion Pages 144

Optimism by *Helen Keller*　　　　　　　　　　　　　　　ISBN: *1-59462-108-X*　**$15.95**
*Helen Keller was blind, deaf, and mute since 19 months old, yet famously learned how to overcome these handicaps, communicate with the world, and
spread her lectures promoting optimism. An inspiring read for everyone...*　　　　Biographies/Inspirational Pages 84

Sara Crewe by *Frances Burnett*　　　　　　　　　　　　　ISBN: *1-59462-360-0*　**$9.45**
*In the first place, Miss Minchin lived in London. Her home was a large, dull, tall one, in a large, dull square, where all the houses were alike, and all the
sparrows were alike, and where all the door-knockers made the same heavy sound...*　　　　Childrens/Classic Pages 88

The Autobiography of Benjamin Franklin by *Benjamin Franklin*　　ISBN: *1-59462-135-7*　**$24.95**
*The Autobiography of Benjamin Franklin has probably been more extensively read than any other American historical work, and no other book of its kind
has had such ups and downs of fortune. Franklin lived for many years in England, where he was agent...*　　　Biographies/History Pages 332

Name	
Email	
Telephone	
Address	
City, State ZIP	

☐ **Credit Card**　　　　　　☐ **Check / Money Order**

Credit Card Number	
Expiration Date	
Signature	

Please Mail to:　Book Jungle
　　　　　　　　　PO Box 2226
　　　　　　　　　Champaign, IL 61825
　　or Fax to:　　630-214-0564

ORDERING INFORMATION

web: *www.bookjungle.com*
email: *sales@bookjungle.com*
fax: *630-214-0564*
mail: *Book Jungle PO Box 2226 Champaign, IL 61825*
or PayPal *to sales@bookjungle.com*

Please contact us for bulk discounts

DIRECT-ORDER TERMS

**20% Discount if You Order
Two or More Books**
Free Domestic Shipping!
Accepted: Master Card, Visa,
Discover, American Express

www.ingramcontent.com/pod-product-compliance
Lightning Source LLC
Chambersburg PA
CBHW080834250626
47160CB00008B/2926